I0622248

Tell Me a Fable

A collection inspired by the Brothers' Grimm

Edited by

A. W. Gifford & Jennifer L. Gifford

Dark Opus Press
P.O. Box 1545
Highland, MI 48357

www.betenoiremagazine.com

Tell Me a Fable is published by Dark Opus Press a division of Charm Noir Omnimedia P.O Box 1545 Highland, MI 48357

This anthology is a work of fiction. Names, characters, places, and scenarios are the products of the authors' imagination. Any resemblance to actual persons living or dead, places, or events is purely coincidental.

Tell Me a Fable © 2013 Charm Noir Omnimedia

Cover art © 2013 L.A. Spooner

All stories © 2013 of their respective creators

ISBN-13: 978-0615944432
ISBN-10: 0615944434

All rights reserved. No portion of this publication can be reproduced by any means without the prior written permission from the authors of the work or Charm Noir Omnimedia

CONTENTS

Introduction

One of the most enduring forms of literature, the fable is timeless in its history as it is important in its literary prose. It's our morality, our history, and a small part of our legacy passed down in written word. It represents the cumulative total of society's morals and ethics. A culture's history of medicine, religion, political and social beliefs can often be found in the fables and fairytales passed down over time.

Found in nearly every culture in every country, the fable is arguably one of the most endearing elements in folklore, encompassing a society's subculture—their legends, oral traditions, customs, superstitions, music, and rituals—into a personal chronicle of historical significance. The fable, in short, represents the silent voice of our social collective consciousness throughout our history.

Set with relevant themes using mythical creatures, animals, plants, and inanimate objects that anthropomorphize into memorable characters to teach a lesson of morals, fables were often used as a means of illustration for societal consequences when ill-gotten behavior and sinful nature ran astray. The fable was meant to guide our moral compass, direct our subconscious towards a greater wisdom in order to live a better life. It highlighted the pitfalls and snares of leading an immoral (and sometimes ungodly) life. It taught that actions have consequences.

Yet it was two brothers, Jacob and Wilhelm Grimm, that captured hearts with their beloved collection of fairytales and fables. *Grimms Märchan*, or The Grimm's Fairytales were a collection of German tales, many of them recorded from the oral tradition, and influenced European culture for centuries. A variable mix of fable, verse, and romanticism, Grimm's Fairytales set the precedence for the literary genre with four simple words: Once Upon a Time. The stories' resiliency and popularity are still prevalent today, cementing their legacy in literary history.

From the books of Timothy and Titus in the New Testament of the bible to Aesop's fables and the stories of Hans Christian Anderson, history is full with literary examples of fables and fairytales meant to educate, instruct, and enlighten. Even modern writers like Tolstoy and Kafka are considered fabulists. George Orwell's novel, *1984*, and the writings of Dr. Seuss, are still using the fable as a metaphor for social commentary, satirizing communal injustices and highlighting that not all fairytales have happy endings.

Grimm's Fairytales hold a special place in the hearts of our editors at Dark Opus Press, and we were excited to launch an anthology that was reflective of our love of fairytales and fables. We wanted a modern telling of Grimm's tales, yet we still wanted to capture the gothic allure and dark lore that is signature of Grimm.

Our personal favorites like The Shroud, Hansel and Gretel, Briar Rose, and Death's Messengers, as well as a few others have been reworked with a modern flare, but the simple truths of their morals have been left untouched. We hope you enjoy the mythical people and places *Tell Me a Fable* will bring you.

And so we start...

Once upon a time...

Jennifer L. Gifford
December, 2013

The Broken

K. Trap Jones

We're known by many names. The whisper of the wind carries the rumors throughout every town, describing us with fictitious elements. There is an aroma of fear that surrounds us, so much so that many refuse to say our name. We have been portrayed as giants, ogres and even dwarfs, but we are none of these. A large bounty has been placed on our heads for the crimes that have been committed. They are justified, but too low in monetary value for our liking. I am the cock and my partner is the hen. Together we are the Broken, the troublemakers of folklore and tall tales.

Our road has been long and the journey has been tiresome. It started harmlessly enough; the hen and I were brought together by a society that saw us as outcasts. My missing feathers proved shameful in the eyes of my flock and the discolored hues of the hen granted him the same. We quickly formed a bond within the tavern as we drank our sorrows away. Hungered from the beer, we sought out to the hillside where the pine nuts were abundant. We talked about our mutual utter disgust towards the judging eyes of society as we gathered the food. We ate everything that we could and gorged ourselves on nature's feast, but we became greedy and collected more than we should. Maybe it was the remnants of the beer or the intoxication from the pine, but we needed to devise some method of carrying the load.

"How about a sled? We could push it down the hill," the hen suggested.

"Too fast; we would never be able to keep up with it," I replied.

"A wagon then; we could pull it."

It was the only idea that made sense; construct a wagon from the sticks and nuts. It wasn't one of our brightest moments, but it actually looked sturdy enough to achieve the goal.

"So who is going to pull it?" I said with a curious tone.

"I thought you were," the cock stated with a sneer.

"You're bigger; you should do it," I said, not given in to his pressure.

We sat there in front of our nut wagon, staring at one another. I could tell that he was trying to outsmart me. Of course, I was trying to do the same in return. While our eyes envisioned the mutilation of each of our corpses, we were interrupted by the sound of fluttering wings.

"What the hell do you two think you're doing?" a duck said, landing in front of our wagon. "These are my damn nuts."

"Claimed nuts? I have never heard of such a thing," I said, bowing up my chest.

"Call it whatever you want, but you bastards aren't taking my nuts."

"So, this whole hilltop is yours?" the hen sarcastically stated.

"And everything on it," the duck proclaimed in a deviant voice.

"You can't be serious. Isn't your place in a pond somewhere?" I asked.

"Listen, we can do this the easy way or the bloody way; your choice."

With the eyes of the duck focused on me, I noticed the hen reaching for a stick. Looking back, it was a turning point for us. We could have easily left the nuts alone and wandered back into town, but in some weird way, we saw the duck as a representative of society. His words were beating us down like all the others. We were tired of the judging eyes; we were tired of not having a voice. The hen gripped the stick with the same vengeance that I had in my thoughts. His feet inched closer.

"And if we don't?" I said, staring directly into the duck's eyes.

"Then I will not stop beating you until the very last nut within your bellies come puking up from your..."

The stick splintered against the back of his head and his tongue spilled out from behind the beak. We only offered a smile of appreciation to one another. The turning point; from then on out, things became interesting.

"So who's pulling the wagon?" the hen asked with a smile.

Everything stalled until the duck woke up. We could barely understand him with the vine rein in his mouth. His wings fluttered about but he was unable to take flight. We had bound him good to the wagon. The only movement he could achieve was walking forward. We each had a large stick that we used to motivate the duck. Blood arced backwards with every strike, but the concept kept us moving. Atop the large mound of nuts in the back, the hen and I sat taking turns pegging the back of the duck's head with rotten nuts that we discovered.

The path was tough due to the mud, but we didn't care. The duck was struggling and losing a large amount of blood, but he was a trooper and kept us going forward.

"Hey! Over here!" a high pitched voice rang out.

I pulled the reins so hard that I damn near tore the duck's head off. On the side of the path was a pin and needle staring at us, waving their arms in a panic. Unfortunately, at the time, I couldn't tell the difference between the two of them.

"Thanks for stopping," the pin stated out of breath.

"Yeah, we didn't think you would," the needle added.

"Who and what the hell are you?" I asked out of curiosity.

"I'm a pin and this is a needle," the pin explained.

"What's the damn difference?" the hen asked.

"Screw you, I could ask you two the same question," the needle replied.

He had a good point. We looked at one another and tried to find a difference between the two of us. A hen and cock; a pin and needle. There was an awkward moment of silence.

"Look dumbass, the needle has an eye; a hole in his freaking head, whereas I don't," the pin explained. "Satisfied?"

The little bastard was correct. It was so obvious, that neither of us realized it.

"Can we get a ride or what?" the pin shouted. "We obviously won't take up too much room and weigh less than one of those nuts you got there."

"Either that or we find you while you sleep and stake your pupils through your eyelids. Trust us; it wouldn't be the first time. There's a reason why we are on the run," the needle threatened.

They climbed aboard as I pulled at the reins to wake up the duck. Groggy and weakened from the blood loss, he continued to pull the wagon forward.

"Is that a duck?" the pin asked.

"Yeah," the hen responded.

"Nice," the needle stated.

The path was long winded and the duck was almost cooked. On the outskirts of town, his lifeless beak fell against the mud. The inn was just up ahead, so we left our wagon and the dead duck on the side of the road. The travel was tiresome and we were thirsty for a beer. The pin and needle tagged along with us.

As the doors swung open, we felt all of those judging eyes of society fall upon us again. The smoked thickened air could not overshadow the stares. The piano playing could not drown out the whispers. The environment made my blood boil and my heart race with anxiety.

"There's a lot of eyes in here that are in need of blinding," the pin stated, looking around.

"Indeed," the needle responded.

Our party of misfits walked up to the bar. The innkeeper ignored us until I pounded my feathered fist on the stained wooden bar.

"I see you; I'm waiting for you to leave," the innkeeper stated, his pig teeth covered in drooling saliva.

"Four beers," I demanded, staring at his disgusting snout.

"We don't serve your kind here."

"And what kind is that?" the hen asked.

"You're broken, I can tell by just looking at you. Outcasts, hoodlums and we don't serve your kind here."

The pin and needle inched forward, but were stopped by my wing.

"How about a trade?" I offered.

"Trade? For what?"

"My buddy here is about to lay an egg," I announced, gesturing towards the wide-eyed hen. "The biggest egg you have ever seen."

I could see more saliva dripping from his mouth. That fat, disgusting pig would not pass up an egg.

"One drink each; nothing more."

He filled up four filthy glasses and went about his business.

"What the hell?" the hen mumbled, underneath his breath.

"Can you even lay eggs?" I responded softly.

"No dumbass, I'm a male."

"Alright, we finish our beer and flee."

About half way through our drinks, the innkeeper walked back up to us.

"Where's the egg?" he slurred.

I could tell he was hungry by the way he kept licking his lips.

"There seems to be a misunderstanding. You see, I didn't realize that my friend here was incapable of laying eggs."

The pig's lips snarled in disappointment. His arms flexed while he scrubbed a glass with a dirty rag. Both the pin and needle stood at attention. Behind us, I heard the chairs squeaking against the saturated wooden floor.

"One of you two feathered assholes better give me an egg or I'll be feasting on something else instead."

A hound dog was breathing down my neck. He was joined by a mule and a goat.

"We don't want any trouble," the hen stated.

"We are well passed what you want," the pig stated.

Everything went so fast; the amount of blood spilled was astonishing. I felt the paw of the hound dog touch my shoulder. I grabbed his wrist and twisted it until it snapped. He howled in pain as the hen sunk his claws into the mule's face. The pen daggered itself within the forehead of the goat while the needle stuck the pig within his left eye. I dove my beak within the skull of the hound dog. So deep, I believe that I could taste his brain. The hen followed the mule down to the ground where he proceeded to violently peck at his face. The needle dislodged itself and fell to the bar before leaping back up, penetrating another portion of the pig's neck.

Within seconds, the whole ordeal was done. Four bodies encompassed us as we finished our drinks. The blood saturated our feathers and glistened against the metal of the pin and needle.

No words were spoken as we sat at the bar; none needed to be said. There had been many turning points within our journey, but for some odd reason, that was not one of them.

Outside, several squirrels were stealing our nuts. They quickly stopped when they noticed the four of us approaching them while drenched in blood.

"We're going to need a new duck," the needle stated.

"I'll find one," the pin replied.

Our personalities had all changed that day and we continued down a path of vengeance and revolution towards the society that had shunned us. Every look of disgust; every act of bullying against us was met with a swift response.

We became an anti-societal symbol of freedom. We were worshipped by all animals that were deemed broken. We were mocked by those that were perfect. Bounty hunters tried their best to stalk us with the hopes of collecting the escalating reward. Each one fell victim to our hatred and despise towards the regulation. We became the voice of folklore; the basis behind legends.

Our tale is embedded within every young mind, but no one knows if we are still alive. Rumors speak of us as ghosts within the forest; a spark within the flame of justice.

We are still alive and our pack will continue to haunt the idealism of perfection within every town that we enter. The winds will provide warnings before our arrival and the moon will predict the bloodshed, but no one is safe from our reach, for we are within the minds of the youth and all of those who have been shunned for having an imperfection.

K. Trap Jones is an author of horror novels and short stories. With a sadistic inspiration from Dante Alighieri and Edgar Allan Poe, he has a temptation towards narrative folklore, classic literary works and obscure segments within society that lead to his raw emotional and often depressive narrative tone dealing with the complications and conflictions of the human mind.

His novel THE SINNER (Blood Bound Books, 2012) won the Royal Palm Literary Award.

He is also a member of the Horror Writer's Association.

EYELESS OLD GOTHEL

Danielle N. Gales

The people are alike to sheep under the watch of the Sisters. Let them not stray, but instead guide them, tend them, minister to them the light of the Saints. If one should run from the light, use only the harshest of methods to bring him to heel, and surely the Saints shall smile upon you for all of your days.

— The Watch of the Sisters, Book Four

They think her a fool, old Gothel. They think her blind to their trespasses — the eyeless woman they call her, yet not all need eyes to see.

It is the dead of night and in her garden something crawls, sneaks, snatches. "Dearest friend", old Gothel would say if only she could speak with her visitor, "surely you had but to ask". After all, is that not what her herbs are there for? Is that not her place? But, ah! Not this one, this one doesn't want to be seen, doesn't want to be found in the sight of eyeless old Gothel. This one, perhaps, keeps dangerous secrets. Whispers of lustful bodies, sinful acts, quickened bellies, held not in the presence of the Saints.

Ugly old Gothel need not be angry, not when she can make the burglar come to her willingly. None know the herbs of her garden better than she: those with leaves that calm the rash, seeds that dull the pain, roots that burn away illness. It is of no moment to exchange those that might ease the birthing of a harlot's bastard with those that cause the blood to run, and leave her sinful interloper none the wiser... for a time.

But when the labour pangs come, when the fruit of their lustful nature arrives in a night of red blood and white pain and black screams, where then can they turn?

Old fool Gothel, they call her. Eyeless old Gothel—her sight, sharp as it ever was.

... and if the spawn of the demon be female it shall not be allowed to remain, but instead shall be taken in at once, lest it also become as its mother. Raise these children and teach them in the light that they may be saved.

— The Watch of the Sisters, Book Seven

Rapunzel she shall be called, after the least of the herbs the thief had stolen. A girl born with sin deep in her heart, just like her mother. Just like old Gothel.

Old Gothel takes the infant, as is the price. The demon wretch mother, see how she begs with her hollow words, how she cries her empty tears for her child. Old Gothel slams the door on her, trapping her inside with her lascivious deceits. Others with keen eyes can watch her close now that the truth of her shame is revealed.

The father—her little sneak-thief—he begs her so. "Must it be this way?" he pleads.

He's tall, this one, his body the product of long, heavy hours under the sun; such strength is but a trifle before the weakness in his soul. Gothel sees him from a great distance before swooping in with her sight, sees the nights he lies with his demon woman, flesh all twisted and glistening and excited and mounting and full and ripe and bursting and, and, and...

Oh, how she hates him.

She sees it and it burns, scolds her deep. Look upon his eyes now, all wet weakness and regret. See how he averts them from her hideousness—her scarred face, her hairless head, the strip of coarse black cloth wrapped where her eyes once sat.

Gothel smiles. "You know the price well enough," she tells him. "Be thankful I'm of a gentle enough temperament to take only the child.

Many amongst the Sisters would not be so kind to your demon woman."

"But what do we do now?"

Oh, how she wants to tell him: *There is no hope for her, or for you as long as you feed her lust.* "Bring the demon woman to the path of righteousness, or set her loose as sport for the dogs."

"Sister Gothel, please," he cries, and now hunched old Gothel seems the taller of them, "will we ever see her again? The child?"

"Never. Wickedness has no future under the eyes of the Saints. Put the child from your thoughts."

And there she leaves him with his demon woman. It would have been a kindness to end them both, she thinks as she steps across tree roots and narrow streams and disappears into the darkened woods. The child squirms in her grasp, cries out. "Hush, child," old Gothel soothes, "tonight you have been saved."

❧

Be not deceived by those fair of appearance, for subterfuge is the mark of the enemy. Even the most innocent must needs be purged of this sickness.

— *The Epigrams of Saint Agromar, Volume Sixteen*

❧

She grows, the child, as does her hair. All of three years and already it is down to her waist, all silken and vibrant and strong, a telltale of the lust sure to one day take root in her heart. Old eyeless Gothel knows. She sees it all.

All of five years and further down it reaches. Old Gothel tries to tame it, she does. Tries to temper it, halt it with the scissors but always it returns quick. Old fool Gothel, she knows it is beyond her power to stop the growth. The child looks sweet and harmless with her fair flowing locks and guileless smiles, yet all of it is a mask, a charade for the darkness lurking within. Only when the child is ready to confront her evil nature will the growth be controlled.

All of seven years and with the ends brushing her feet, Rapunzel is filled with questions, a burning desire to know. Old Gothel answers as she can, educating the child in the ways of goodness.

"Why, 'amma," young Rapunzel asks some days, "don't you have any hair?"

"Because, dear child, the Saints demand it of me, as they very well might of you one day."

"But I like my hair," Rapunzel says. "Doesn't it make me pretty?"

"Oh, very much so," Gothel answers with a frown. "But your mother was pretty too, and you remember what I taught you about her."

"I don't understand," the girl pouts, striking the ground with a petulant foot. "Tris says I'm pretty, and he's nice to me."

Ah. The troublesome boy from the neighbouring farm. Now that is something eyeless old Gothel shall have to watch with care. At such a tender age it begins, like a single loose thread ripping a garment asunder, teasing, tantalising at first but then exposing the flesh beneath and filling the body with a pulsing desire. Such threads must be stitched early.

All of ten years and Rapunzel sings to him, that troublesome boy, enraptures him with her honeyed melodies. But where did she learn such songs? Where did she hone her siren's voice? Surely it is as the Saints have said: *The evil wells up within, unseen. It takes many forms for a quick escape, and then follows the corruption.* Old Gothel forbids her, yet still the girl's voice intrudes upon a night's quiet, reaching, yearning, prying, scattering about all of its tasty little seeds for strangers to fall upon unawares.

All of eleven years and petulant the girl grows. Away she sneaks in the day and the night, hair weaving a trail like a snake in the long grass, her bite far more subtle but just as poisonous. The places Rapunzel goes old Gothel daren't imagine, and so Gothel locks the doors and bars the windows. The girl is not to walk alone, not to be trusted. Yet she fights old Gothel so, and finally Gothel is left with but one option, one solution to set the girl on the path of light.

Amongst those most depraved, none stand lower than woman. She is a savage beast, a blight upon the men of the earth, the beginning and the end of mortal toil. For this reason, the select few women amongst you — those most turned to the light — must stand watch against your own kind. For it is written that only a beast may understand a beast.

— Commands of the Lords Paramount

All of twelve years, and it is to the tower Rapunzel must go.

The tower is ugly, crumbling, forgotten. There are no doors, no stairs, no secrets beyond those Gothel shares in. Up the tall ladder they go and through the window, the only way in or out. Once in, old Gothel kicks the ladder to the ground. It won't be needed any longer.

"But 'amma, how long must I remain in this tower?" the girl protests.

"Why, you can leave whenever you are ready. By then, you will know how." Crafty old Gothel, sneaky, deceitful, treacherous old snake. Sometimes she suspects her woman's dark soul could be her greatest ally, though she'd never give voice to such thoughts amongst the other Sisters.

"I don't understand," Rapunzel cries. "Why must I stay here?"

"For the quiet. For the contemplation. Many hours the day has, all yours now to study the words of the Saints, free of distraction." The room is already stocked with all that the girl needs: the shrine to the Saints, the volumes containing their words, the small bed and dresser, and the full-length mirror—most important, Gothel knows, for when the girl is truly ready to begin her journey.

"But I already study the Saints, just as you tell me to!" the girl protests.

"Do you think the Saints smile upon those who make hollow mockeries of their words like mindless little songbirds? It is not enough! You must feel it in your heart. Look at yourself in that mirror. Go on, look hard, my girl. Do you see something worthy of the Saints' light?"

There the girl stands, her full height reflected, the quivering of her lips, the doubt in her eyes thrown back at her. "I... I want to walk in the light. I wish I weren't so rotten."

Old Gothel is not without pity, no, not without warmth. She touches the girls shoulder, stands at her side, both now reflected. "My dear, what you are is not your fault; that falls upon your wretched mother. Nonetheless, you are what you are, and so you must struggle the harder for your salvation."

"I... I want to be good, I..." And now Rapunzel stands tall, lips firm, eyes steel, and Old Gothel delights—there is hope yet. "I will make myself worthy, I swear it so."

"Good. Then I shall be away," Gothel says.

"I'm to be all alone?"

"Well I shall visit, of course. Listen for my call, and then use the window hook to let down your hair, so that I might climb it." Old Gothel beckons the girl over to the window.

"My hair? But that sounds awfully painful. Couldn't you use the ladder again?"

"I could, my dear, but it is only through pain that we learn and grow." Ah, but old Gothel knows the girl's tricks, knows her deceits. It is not pain that frightens Rapunzel, no, but something far more vain. It is that hair of hers that she loves, the source of her pride, of her evil. Look at how she trembles, see how she fears for her beauty. "Now, could you please?"

And so the girl leans over, takes her voluminous hair and wraps it tight around the hook, before tossing the rest from the window. Old Gothel climbs down with care, each handhold accompanied by a squeal from the window. Old Gothel's heart is heavy; she does not enjoy what she does, no, but it must be done all the same. The sun will rise in the west before old Gothel sees the girl become her mother.

So the years pass and Rapunzel stays confined to her tower. Old Gothel comes twice daily, once to bring the girl's breakfast and once to bring her dinner. She arrives at the tower's base and gives out her call: "Rapunzel! Rapunzel! Let down your hair!"

All of sixteen and see how pretty she is. Yes, pretty with her hair, pretty in her dresses, pretty, pretty. See how she admires her beauty in the mirror in her pretty clothes; see how the girl becomes the temptress. Old Gothel steers her away, feeds her the purging roots with her food. Beautiful Rapunzel, see how pretty she is now in front of her mirror with her pretty clothes all soiled and her face all wretched with bile.

"That is what beauty makes of us, my dear," ugly old Gothel teaches. "Beauty is a sickness, a foul ploy. Steer yourself away from it. Drown your pride."

"Yes, 'amma," the girl struggles between heaves, "I understand, 'amma."

Ah, does she truly? Sure enough she swaps her pretty clothes for the bland roughspun woollens that plain old Gothel favours, and sure enough in her visits old Gothel sees the girl in prayer or hunched over the books, devouring the lessons of the Saints. But, but...

All of seventeen and still the girl sings. She sings from her window in the sun, she sings from her bed in the moonlight, always old Gothel hears her siren's call. Each night a song, and each morning a mouthful of salt, as it should be—old Gothel will purify the girl's tongue one way or another, she will. Yet it is to no avail—the singing continues in defiance of old Gothel's lessons. She worries so, old Gothel does, that this dark obsession with song shall be the girl's undoing; that all of her hard work and years in dedication to saving this soul will be for naught.

"But sinful lives are freer", the spider told Saint Veynan. "There's a beauty in chaos, a freedom in anarchy", it spoke. "Come close now, so I might enlighten you."

I tell you now, sin is a tangled web, a thing of beauty from a distance, so alluring, so appealing that the unwary can't help but be drawn in close to admire its intricacy, the ways the delicate structures all lace together and create the whole.

Be wary, for always the spider watches and waits...

— The Trials of Saint Veynan

She sings from her tower and the stranger is drawn close, old Gothel knows. Treacherous old Gothel.

He stands at the base of the tower and calls to her, "Rapunzel, Rapunzel, let down your hair!"

And so she does, fool girl. Down her hair stretches and up the man climbs. Gothel knows what passes within. Day by day the stranger returns, gives out his call, makes the climb. Hours they spend together, the girl thinking her 'amma none the wiser, but eyeless old Gothel sees all.

What schemes do they concoct within? What lusts grow between them, Rapunzel and her fair prince? They think to escape together, perhaps, yet for all her sin the girl's growing devotion to the Saints holds true. She won't leave, mustn't leave, lest her evil nature overtake her.

And yet, and yet... Ever they draw closer, Rapunzel and her fair prince. It is in her hair where her pride lies, and so her man runs his fingers through the lengths, whispers in her ear of her beauty, of her irresistibility, and finally she can take no more. Yes, yes, she will go with him! They will contrive to escape together deep in the night while old fool Gothel sleeps. Later he will return with a sturdy ladder to carry them both to safety; this very night it must be, before poor 'amma suspects.

But eyeless old Gothel sees all.

She waits for the fair prince to depart, and then she calls to the girl: "Rapunzel, Rapunzel, let down your hair!"

Up old Gothel climbs, hands gripping the wicked hair. Within the tower Rapunzel unwraps her hair from the hook and stands for all the world like a portrait of innocence, but old Gothel confronts her with her sin, watches as the girl collapses into a sobbing wreck on the floor.

"I'm sorry, 'amma, I— I—" the girl cries, trapped by the workings of her own lust.

"You are weak and foolish!" old Gothel yells.

"I am weak and foolish, 'amma. Sinful. Evil."

"Yes! Now you understand what you are, the danger you represent."

"But what can I do?" Rapunzel pleads, tears streaking her face and ruining her eyes.

"Get up off that floor for one. The Saints have no respect for a pitiful wretch."

"Oh, the Saints!" the girl cries as she struggles to her feet. "The Saints will forsake me."

"The Saints forsake none who defy the evil in their soul. Tell me, what evil lurks in yours?"

"I... I don't know."

"Then think, girl! Think! What is it about you that most drives the sin? What ensnared the man so?"

"My singing, that's what brought him."

"That is what brought him, but what was it that entrapped him?"

"He... He said my beauty was irresistible, like an angel."

"Yes, yes. But more than this, what is the source of his desire?" The girl knows, the girl knows, but see how she fears the truth of it. Old Gothel must walk with her these important steps, lead her to the edge, give her the push she so needs. "What about you did he find most tempting? What amongst his honeyed words in your ears made you falter, helped the demon within your heart break free?"

"I... He said..." There Rapunzel's words fall into nothing, her face drawn, her gaze searching the room, finally falling upon a thin object glinting upon the dresser. A pair of scissors.

"Good," Gothel says. "Now you know what you must do."

Rapunzel snatches the scissors and then, her steps awash with purpose, she moves before the mirror.

"Defy the demon within you," old Gothel pushes, "defy it!"

The girl faces the mirror with the scissors in her hand, and with her other she grabs a handful of her hair and holds it out straight. But then... then she hesitates, eyes flashing this way and that, lip quivering, scissors held loose. Old Gothel waits, watches, doesn't interfere. She knows now is the time for steel, and after a moment, so does the girl.

"I defy it." Her eyes narrow and her lips draw into a straight, determined line, and then she hacks at the hair with the scissors and great tides collapse to the floor. On she goes, the scissors cutting swathes right quick and close to her flesh. Again and again, sharp steel slashes until all that remains are jagged, patchy tufts on her scalp. On the floor it all lays, like a python finally slain. Rapunzel's breath is ragged, her hand around the scissors not quite ready to admit the task is over with.

Gothel places a gentle hand on her shoulder. "Now, my sweet, you are ready to go."

"Go?" the girl asks, her breath ragged. "I... can leave?"

"There is a place for you at the College of the Sisters, just as there was for me when I was of your age." And much she has to learn there. The cutting of her hair was merely the beginning.

"You speak true?" See her now, awash with relief, excitement sparkling in her eyes. "But there are no doors to this tower, no stairs. How are we to leave?"

"You tell me."

Then the girl thinks for a moment, before her gaze falls upon the trail of her sinful beauty upon the floor. Rapunzel takes one end of the cuttings and ties them into a firm knot. Dragging the shorn silken hair across the floor, she attaches the knotted end to the window hook and throws the remainder from the window and down the side of the tower.

Old Gothel grins. "My dear, now you see: the way out was always before you."

By day's end Rapunzel is gone, sent off to the care of the Sisters. Old Gothel knows not to feel sad; this is all she had ever wanted for the girl. Back to her home she will go, back to her garden to tend the villagers with their cruel tongues. Yet first, there is one more thing she must do.

Old Gothel meets with Rapunzel's fair prince, counts out the coins into his eager palms, watches as he stuffs them greedily away.

She looks upon him now: his handsome face, his wolfish grin, his muscular physique. Look at the sureness in his step, the arrogance. Her heart flutters some at the feel of him. Much like her young love, many years past. She remembers the taste of his breath, the feel of his chest as her fingers dawdled across his muscles, the way her nerves leapt when he gazed upon her with those eyes...

Wicked Gothel. Bad, lustful, low Gothel.

It had been such thoughts that had caused her to put out her own eyes many years past rather than stir the temptation in her sinful heart. Even that much had been fruitless when the second sight came to her. She'd never escape her base nature. None of them could. They had to be taught the hardest way.

He looks upon her ugly scarred face now and he sneers, pities. Oh, but if only he knew. In her younger days her beauty had been unsurpassed, or so she'd been told. The men flocked to her, and in their eyes lay neither pity nor disgust. She'd felt helpless before them, and so had done the only thing she could. She had taken her face to a vat of boiling water. In that scalding crucible she revelled in her own anguish, felt the purifying light of the Saints fill her body as her beauty was stripped away. Clean, she emerged from that water. Clean. One day soon, Rapunzel will face her own test.

Yes, she thinks, this one was a good investment. A costly one, but the sinful must be confronted with their nature.

Always must you struggle with the demon in your heart, as surely as it struggles against you. If your hair be lustrous and long, take to it the blade. If your face be marked by extraordinary beauty, mark it instead with fire. If your eyes should betray you and threaten temptation, have them out at once. Discover the sin and purge it! Purge it from your flesh, from your mind, from your soul. Only then, dear Sister, shall you walk in the light.

— The Watch of the Sisters, Book One

Rapunzel writes to eyeless old Gothel from the College. She does well, the girl says. The Sisters are harsh, more by far than old Gothel. The girl misses her 'amma, and knows now why her upbringing had to be the way it was. She found her courage and her strength, she writes. She walks in the light of the Saints now.

One morning early in the sun's light Rapunzel sang quietly as was her way, and yet at that moment caught sight of herself in the mirror, caught the reflection of her sin. She thought of her 'amma, thought of her scarred, eyeless face and of the sacrifices the Saints demanded, and all at once she knew. Her songs have fallen silent now, laid low by the strike of the hot sharp blade that sliced away her tongue.

Old Gothel hopes the Saints will forgive her, for she is proud; proud as surely as her own 'amma had been of her in her youth. Her brave girl Rapunzel, now she understands.

The ignorant people, they will never understand the sacrifices the Sisters make for their protection. Old fool Gothel, they call her, but more fool them. *See there the eyeless woman,* they say in hushed tones as she passes, yet they are the ones who are blind. Beastly creature they say, evil, wicked, bad, lustful, low old Gothel, and in all of that they have the truth of it... But they should feel gladness in their hearts, for it is written that only a beast may understand a beast.

ॐ

Danielle N. Gales *is a writer from Sunny Hastings, UK. When she isn't reading or writing speculative fiction of all varieties, she spends too much time playing video games, fattening her rats with treats, and drinking way too much coffee. Her fiction has also appeared or is upcoming in* Kazka

BREAD CRUMBS

Wendy N. Wagner

Hank peered around the corner of the deserted kite shop, keeping a ragged display of wind socks between himself and the parking lot. Nothing moved except the blinking of the bakery's Christmas lights. Over the constant stink of seawater and rotting fish, the smell of fresh bread drifted toward him.

His stomach growled.

Greta yanked him down by the backpack strap. "Did you see anything?" Her blue eyes looked huge on her thin face, and he knew she was just as hungry as he was.

He opened his mouth to answer, but Greta stiffened. She had her slingshot out of her pocket before he could even figure out what she'd heard. Behind him, a soft squawk and a thud: she'd hit a seagull. She rolled under the boardwalk railing and stomped its throat with a vicious crunch. It flopped once and went still.

It was hard to believe that just a month ago Greta's biggest worry had been making first chair clarinet.

Greta scrambled up beside Hank. He patted her knee. "Thanks." She was so much better at hearing the seagulls. They weren't as big a problem as the fish-frog men, but the seashore creatures all seemed to communicate between themselves.

His stomach growled again, loud enough for Greta to hear. "Did you see anything?" she repeated. She was probably hungrier than him. One can of scavenged Pringles wasn't enough food to get two teenagers through the day. They'd planned to dig clams, but there were just too many seagulls out on the beach this morning.

He wondered about that. Had the sea creatures caught on to them? After all, they had to be the last humans left in Sunset Bay. He folded his arms around his grumbling belly as if his arms could muffle its sounds. For the first time in days, he let himself wish his mother were here. She would know what to do. She would know if this was a trap or a genuine opportunity to fill his aching stomach.

"It just doesn't feel right. They have Christmas lights on. That means ... electricity."

"Maybe they've got a generator."

"Come on, Grets. Generators run on gas and those ... *things* have all the gas."

"What do monsters need with gasoline, anyway?" she mused.

"To keep us from driving, I guess. Mom said —" Hank broke off. He didn't want to think about his mother.

Greta rubbed her arms. "It's getting colder."

She was right. The wind had changed, driving moisture off the ocean. He ducked down so he could see between the rows of shops and out over the tops of the moored boats. A fog bank hung heavy at the edge of the horizon. They didn't have much time to get back to the house before the fog swallowed the little beach town.

He closed his eyes a second. The persistent hunger headache made it hard to think clearly. "Okay, we'll just case the place, look through the windows. If we see anything fishy, we run for it."

Greta jumped to her feet. "I'll take this side. You take the other. You're faster."

Hank tightened his backpack straps, shot her a thumbs-up, then jumped the fence, streaking across the parking lot. He didn't slow until he hit the cover of the spindly pine trees flanking the bakery's side. Greta hustled toward her own assignment.

Up close, the smell made his head spin. He had to wipe actual drool off his chin. He hadn't smelled anything that good since the sea things showed up.

He rounded the corner. The Christmas lights on this side of the bakery didn't blink. Their steady multi-colored glow lit the artificial icicles like a hazy rainbow or the Northern Lights. It left Hank more exposed than he'd normally risk, but damn it, the smell. Any risk was worth taking to get close to that smell.

He pressed his cheek to the window frame and peered in through layers of garland. A table sat in the middle of the room, and a loaf of bread sat on top of the table. No movement though, and no fish-frogs. He licked his lips.

On the other side of the building, glass smashed.

Hank somersaulted away from the window.

Greta.

He had to hurry.

Behind him, a familiar laugh sounded. He turned to see Greta open the window and stick her head out. Tinsel sparkled in her hair.

"There's nobody here, silly. I'll open the door for you."

His heart felt too big for his chest, thumping away twice its normal speed. "No. Just grab the bread and get out of there."

"There's lots of neat stuff in here. You should come check it out."

He shook his head. "Anybody could have heard that noise. We should get the bread and get moving."

She shrugged. "Suit yourself."

The window slid closed, its streamers of garland obliterating his view of his sister. He thought about peeking through it just to see if Greta took anything else, but decided to trust her. She could be reckless, but she wasn't crazy.

He met her at the edge of the parking lot, a loaf of bread tucked under each arm. His stomach rumbled, loud enough Greta's lips twitched in a smirk.

"Maybe we should eat a little before we take off," she suggested. "Over by the kite shop—that spot has pretty good sight lines."

They trotted across the parking lot, watching out for seagulls. But other than the creeping fog bank, they were alone.

Greta ripped a loaf in half, giving Hank one section and keeping the other. She brought the bread to her nose, sniffing her way down the length. "So delicious," she murmured.

Hank rolled his eyes at the drama. "I could have at least used my pocketknife to slice it." But she ignored him, and he couldn't resist cramming his own uncut portion into his mouth. The crust resisted his teeth, but the middle was all fluff. He licked salt off his lips. Whoever baked this loaf, they'd brushed the top with butter, just like his mom used to.

He couldn't help but picture the baker then, a figure in a white apron brushing flour off her hands. Dipping her pastry brush into the stick of butter softening on the counter and smiling down at the little boy sitting at her feet. He knew he was conflating memories with imagination, but he couldn't help himself. His head dropped back against the wall of the kite shop, too heavy to hold up. He tried to blink. Managed to open his eyes. Greta studied the crumb of the chunk of bread in her fingers and smiled at it.

Hank's eyelids sank. His head weighed too much, but somehow it swirled on his shoulders, like it had that New Year's Eve he'd snuck a glass of champagne. His tongue stuck to the roof of his mouth, dry as bread.

Bread.

Oh, shit. The bread.

"I think—" It was so hard to talk.

Greta raised an eyebrow. "You okay, bro?" She brushed the chunk of bread against her nose and giggled.

"Think there's something...wrong..."

"You really sound funny."

"...wrong with this bread."

But she was already chewing, and his eyelids wouldn't stay up any longer.

In the darkness, the smell of baking bread was even stronger.

ᴄᴧᴐ

"Hank, wake up!" Something hard jabbed him in the shoulder over and over again, but it was Greta's voice that dragged him out of unconsciousness.

"Grets?" His throat caught around the words, as scratchy as the bottom of a scouring pad. He leaned closer to her and felt his forehead hit something metal. His eyes were gummy, and he had to blink a few seconds to make sense of what he saw in the dim light.

He sat in a cage, an iron padlock dangling off the front. The cage bars were far enough apart to fit most of his face through, but he could tell they were sturdy. He reached for Greta and realized his right hand was caught in some kind of shackle, attached to a long chain. He tugged it. It didn't even shift.

"What's going on?"

"I don't know. I woke up a few minutes ago, and you were in there. And I feel funny."

"We must have been drugged, something in the bread."

She scratched the top of her hand. "I'm itchy all over, and thirsty, too. What kind of drug does that?"

The top of her hand looked raw and damp, sticky plasma oozing from the scratches she'd left. "Just don't scratch it, okay?" Hank bit his lip, thinking. For now, he felt fine, except for stiff legs and a dry mouth. He looked around himself.

A lantern gave off a dull orange glow on the far side of the dank little space, which Hank's cage dominated. His backpack lay on a stack of industrial-sized bags of flour that leaned against a flight of stairs and one wall. A few crates of potatoes and powdered milk filled the other corner of the room, all ordinary baking stuff. Outside the glow of the lantern, darkness hid the door they'd heard, as well as anyone who might have come in.

"How long have I been asleep?" he asked.

"A couple of hours. I don't think I ate as much bread as you. I—"

But the sound of a door slamming cut her off. Then he heard footsteps on the stairs, and worse, a pair of voices, low and strange, the consonants strangely twisted and muffled as if the speakers' tongues and lips were too squishy to enunciate properly. The speakers came into the light, and Hank had to cover his mouth to keep from crying out.

The baker—it had to be the baker, given the apron tied around its middle—came first, hunchbacked and grinning. Or at least Hank thought it was a grin; it was hard to tell, given the way the flesh peeled back from its broad, slimy lips, as if the skin was no better attached than a loose scab. Then he saw: the skin wasn't attached. The thing wore a human face over its own froggish head like a skier wore a balaclava. He could even smell the faint stench of flesh gone bad. He shuddered. Greta's fingernails dug into his wrist.

The second looked worse. Smelled worse, too. The stink of low tide dripped off it like the water dripping off its clothes. The tan trench coat may have once been a good disguise, but the water-logged face above its collar wouldn't have fooled a blind man. The eye holes sagged, showing the scales and slimy membranes of a fish-man.

"This is a good one," the thing in the trench coat burbled.

The baker nodding, hunching lower to peer into Hank's cage. "Thick skin on it. Perfect for the pilot."

"You sure? The hide looks a bit dry." Trench Coat slipped a webbed hand into the cage, patting Hank's cheek. "Quite dry. Malnourished, I presume."

It pulled back its hand, but not before Hank saw the ragged ends of the human flesh hanging out the end of its coat sleeves. He wiped his cheek on his shoulder.

"A few days of quality fats in his food should soften the hide," the baker assured the fishy thing. It grinned, showing rows of small, sharp teeth. "It is a greedy little creature, not like the other."

"Hey!" Greta jumped to her feet with a metallic jangle. Hank hadn't noticed the collar around her neck. Any further protest she would have made cut off in a sharp bark, and she toppled back onto the ground.

The creature in the trench coat chuckled. "What a wonderful puppy you have acquired, Wanda. I think it will serve you well."

"As long as it serves the bigger one, that's all I care about." The baker nudged Greta with a flour-covered flipper-foot. "We've only got a few days to ready the suit. The pilot's body is close to the change now, and he will need human hands to steer the ship."

Trench Coat beckoned at the baker and they moved toward the stairs. "Speaking of the change, you look like you're advancing rather rapidly yourself. Have you considered finding a second hide to stimulate your decaying human DNA?"

Hank's mind spun as the pair disappeared from his view. Why had the pair captured him and Greta? And why were they wearing human skins? The other fish-frogs never had.

"Hank, did you notice how human these ones seemed to act? And the thing in the trench coat even called the baker 'Wanda.'" Greta rubbed at her throat, working her fingers beneath the rough leather collar as best she could.

"They do seem like people. I've never heard the others talk." He crossed and re-crossed his legs. He wanted to stretch them, or better yet, stand, but there wasn't room in the cage.

"The one said something about decaying human DNA. Do you think they used to *be* people?"

"I don't know what to think. Except that we have to get out of here. I'm scheduled to become a skin suit, and I wouldn't trust *Wanda* not to get attached to your hide, either."

Greta scratched absently at her cheek. "If I could reach your backpack, I could use your pocket knife to pick our locks."

He rested his chin on the cross bar of his cage, studying the heavy iron lock. It looked ancient, crafted years ago by some security-minded blacksmith determined his work would hold up to the toughest crowbar. Even the screws holding the faceplate onto its base looked tough, their cross-marked faces sullenly guarding the keyhole.

"Greta," Hank said slowly, "I've got an idea."

꒰ꔛ꒱

Hank's pocketknife scraped inside the lock. "Are you sure this will work?" Greta paused to scrub the back of her hand over the gash in her neck. The bleeding showed no sign of slowing, and Hank hoped her tetanus shots were up to date. The lock's screws didn't look very clean, but at least they had cut through her collar.

"I hope so." He crossed his fingers as he'd said it. He'd never picked a lock before and neither had Greta. It worked in the movies, but he knew they'd left movie territory behind a long time ago, when the fish-frog men took over the harbor's refueling station and people started disappearing. In the movies, monsters never had plans.

"Do you think this is happening outside of Oregon?" he mused.

"This fish-frog thing?" She shrugged and wiggled the knife back and forth. "I guess so. There sure haven't been any planes flying overhead lately."

But the sound of the door opening above interrupted her. Her eyes widened.

"Hellooo, children. I have something special for the little man," Wanda cooed from above. A wonderful smell, sweet and spicy like gingerbread, wafted down the stairs.

Hank grabbed the pocketknife to still its scratching. He whispered: "Climb up on the flour, like we talked about. Quick!"

Greta ran. In seconds, she'd scrambled up on the flour sacks, with only her feet showing within the circle of the lantern's light. Hank craned his neck, but the horrible clatter told him everything he needed to know. She'd tripped the creature, just as planned.

It lay groaning at the bottom of the stairs. Greta hopped down to the floor and gave it a kick in the ribs. It made a low, burbling sound, like a groan deep underwater.

"Grets, I think it's immobilized."

She kicked it again. "That's for taking my mom."

Hank closed his eyes and an image of his mother filled them, looking just as he'd seen her last. The details were perfect: the pair of tiny pearls that dangled from her ears, the eggplant colored suit. He hadn't even hugged her the morning she disappeared, just waved goodbye with his mouth full of cereal.

He opened his eyes. "Check its pockets for keys so I can out of here and kick it, too."

She dropped to her knees and lifted a victorious, jingling hand. "Got 'em!" She stood up, then swayed. "I feel a little funny."

"It'll be okay." He hoped he wasn't lying.

She worked a big black key into the lock until it clicked. The keys slipped out of her fingers. "Oops." She giggled and fumbled with the keys, looking for the shackle key. Hank knocked the padlock off the cage and pushed the door open. The creature on the floor coughed.

"Hurry up, Greta!"

"I'm a-hurrying." She giggled again and tried one of the smaller keys in the shackle. It didn't fit. "A-hurrying, a-hurrying." She crinkled her nose. "Hey, do you smell fish?"

"Just focus. Try that one."

She slid it home, and the shackle popped off. Hank crawled out of the cage. He slung his pack on his back. "Let's go!"

"Yes, master." Greta laughed, harder this time, and Hank had to pull her to her feet.

The thing on the floor flopped onto its back. "You think you're getting away," it croaked, "but the pilot is coming. He will sail the ship to open the very gates of R'lyeh! Our lord will rise from the depths!"

Greta swayed, and Hank barely caught her. Her eyes rolled up in her head. "Shit."

The thing laughed. "While you were sleeping, I gave her the great gift of Cthulhu. It won't be long before she makes her change, not long at all."

Greta's skin felt cool and moist. Her eyelids flickered.

"Fuck you," Hank growled. He snatched up the lantern. "You took my mom and now you're going to *change* my sister? I don't think so."

From the top of the stairs—struggling not to drop Greta—he tossed the lantern onto the bags of flour. It would take a few minutes for the bags to catch, but they would, sure enough. And maybe the explosion would distract the other fish-frog men long enough for him to get Greta someplace safe.

At the top of the stairs, a million Christmas lights twinkled and danced. He dragged Greta out the storefront and down the stairs, running as fast as he could. Out on the marina, the lights of a hundred fishing boats flashed in their own watery Yuletide. Last night, he'd seen a boat or two, but this was different. They were massing.

He picked up speed, and behind him, something roared. He toppled over, but dragged himself up, Greta slipping out of his arms. She felt more slippery, colder. But he wrenched her back up and kept moving. The air smelled wonderfully of wood smoke and scorched sugar.

Frog-fish things raced past him, but he kept running, and the creatures were focused on the fire. He rounded a corner and slid into their driveway. There was no one behind him when he threw open the front door.

He slid down onto the cool hardwood floor. Greta sniffled. Her lips looked thicker, grayer. He laid his palm on her forehead. It felt cold and damp.

"I don't know what to do," he whispered. "Mom, I wish you were here." He blinked away tears. He couldn't cry. He was all Greta had.

Not for the first time, he wondered if he should load up into the old Suburban and take off for someplace else. Before the radio had gone out, there had been reports of fish-frogs in Portland, but maybe the desert would be safer. There was still plenty of gas left in the tank—

he'd barricaded the Suburban in the garage to protect it from the frog-fish men's siphons. They were always stealing the gas from untended cars.

He slapped his head. "I'm an idiot."

Gas. That's what this was all about. If they were building an armada and a ship to rescue their lord, they'd need fuel. And of course, they wouldn't want anyone to stop them, so they'd need to make sure no one else had any gas, either. He remembered what Greta had said: "There haven't been any planes flying overhead lately."

He brushed his fingertips across Greta's cheek. It felt slick and tender, like frog skin. The baker had given her something to change her into one of them. And if it was that easy to make fish-frog men, then he had to imagine the world was full of them. Full of horrible, slimy creatures waiting to turn the whole planet over to some under-sea lord.

But first they had to find him, and for that, they needed a pilot. They needed a ship. And they needed gas.

Hank grinned. He had an idea.

He left Greta in the tub with the faucet dripping. She might be turning into a frog creature, but she was still his sister, and he wanted her to be comfortable without him. He couldn't really be sure if he would be able to come back to help her.

The fog had finally settled over the town, thick blankets of it, fragrant with sea salt and smoke. Nothing moved in the silence of the night. Even the seagulls perched in stillness, their heads under their wings. Hank crept through the streets, stepping and breathing as quietly as he could.

The docks appeared more quickly than he'd expected. The planks creaked as the waves moved them, a sound he'd always liked. The fuel tanks hunkered right in front of him.

He swallowed hard, and slipped his backpack off his shoulders. He took out his heavy duty flashlight and switched it on. There was the rope and the long-nosed barbecue lighter. His fingers trembled as he unscrewed the lid on the top of the fuel tank. It was a long rope, but he wasn't sure how fast it would burn once it started wicking up gasoline.

Something touched his shoulder. Something damp and cold.

"Hank, what are you doing?"

He didn't want to turn around, but he had to.

Here in the shadows of the fuel tanks, it was hard to make out the fish-frog's features, but he could smell the rank stink of uncured flesh and knew it wore a suit of human skin. It stepped closer to him, still gripping his shoulder with its clammy paw.

"Hank, where's Greta?"

Two white beads caught the glow of the flashlight, swinging like pearls suspended from a pair of ears. His breath caught in his throat.

"I've been looking for you two, you know. And I'm so happy to see you. But I've got to give you a gift before we can be together again."

It stepped closer, and he could see its face now, the cold slimy flesh showing in the sagging eyeholes of a yellowing hide. It wore a long raincoat that he didn't recognize, but the pearl earrings were unmistakable.

He closed his eyes and felt the webbed paw stroke his neck. His stomach clenched. There could be no more hideous a feeling than that unnatural touch.

"I'm sorry," he whispered, and brought up the Maglite, high above the stinking head, and for a horrible moment he thought the creature (*Mom*, something treacherous inside him whispered) would grab his arm. But then the Maglite struck home with a loud thud, and the thing toppled over the edge of the dock.

A soft sploosh broke the silence of the night.

Trembling, Hank threaded the rope into the tank. Without Greta, without his mother, he was lost now, well and truly lost. Maybe he should have let that thing turn him into a fish-frog and been done with it all. He rested his head on the fuel tank for a second, and remembered the stink of the uncured skin suit.

No. He couldn't live like that. Even being alone was better than that. Even being dead was better than that.

Lights flashed at the end of the dock: someone was coming. He didn't have much time.

He reached for the barbecue lighter, and his fingers touched something soft at the bottom of his backpack. A piece of bread. If he made it out of here alive, he would eat every last crumb.

A seagull shrieked overhead. Webbed feet slapped against wooden planks. Wings battered his shoulders and the top of his head.

Hank locked his elbow around the leg of the fuel tank and clicked the lighter's trigger. The flame looked absurdly small. He had to shield it from the seagull's flapping.

"Get him!" something bellowed in gurgling voice.

The end of the rope sizzled. A tendril of smoke rose up. The seagull slashed at his cheek. Hank swatted at it, but its beak flashed again, jabbing into his cheek.

Wet hands grabbed Hank's shoulders and tossed him aside. He slid across the dock, coming up hard against a mooring cleat. With a burst of searing pain, something at his side crunched.

"You can't hurt my boy," his mother blurbled. There was almost nothing human about her, but he would have recognized the steel in her voice anywhere. He'd heard it used at more than one parent-teacher conference. She snatched the seagull out of the air and tossed it aside.

The grunting, gurgling figures reached his mother. She punched one in the face and sent it sprawling.

An amber glow caught Hank's eye. The rope was really burning now, a beautiful yellow flame running up its length. He dragged himself to his feet. "Mom! Run!"

She roared an answer. Whatever humanity remained in her, it was beyond speech. He stumbled back a few steps. The tank was going to blow any second now.

A hand closed on his elbow. He gasped and spun around.

"We've got to get out of here," Greta croaked. Her skin hung in gray shreds, scales glistening in the light of the fish-men's armada. She yanked him toward dry land.

With an impossible loud *whoomp*, the gas tank caught.

Hank hit the side of a Dumpster and slid down. The world had gone silent. The searing white burned his eyes until he closed them. He sat in darkness for a small eternity.

He didn't even move when he felt small hands pull him up to a seating position. It wasn't until she shook his shoulders and slapped his cheek that he opened his eyes. Greta looked even more serious as a fish-girl than she did as a nervous middle schooler.

She pointed sternly back toward the house. He let her help him to his feet. They didn't speak a word as they tore the plywood off the garage door and climbed into the Suburban.

Greta stopped half-in, half-out of the big vehicle. Tears flashed in her enormous eyes. Hank followed her gaze to the brown paper bag sitting on the bench seat.

"Groceries," he breathed. How had he forgotten that his mother had just come back from the grocery store before she left for that meeting? How could he have forgotten that?

Greta lifted out a white plastic-wrapped rectangle. The familiar red-blue-and-yellow logo stood out under the plaintive yellow of the car's dome light.

"Wonderbread."

They slipped into their seats and started the engine.

Wendy N. Wagner's *short fiction has appeared in* Beneath Ceaseless Skies *and the anthologies* Armored *and* The Way of the Wizard. *Her first novel,* Skinwalkers, *is a Pathfinder Tales adventure due out February 2014. An avid gardener and fan of the sweet science, she lives with her family in Portland, Oregon. You can keep up with her at* http://winniewoohoo.com.

Red

Kristal Stittle

Once upon a time, there lived a young girl in a glass and concrete tower, surrounded by rotting monsters.

Her name was Angela and she clearly remembered the day that it happened; the day the dead stopped dying. It had been a year, maybe a year and a half, but it always seemed like yesterday. It had been a big day. The first manned mission to mars was finally returning. Sure, it wasn't as huge as when they had landed there in the first place, but it was still a big day. Angela's class had been learning about the solar system at the time, so their teacher had brought in one of the TVs and they got to watch the live feed. Angela didn't go to class anymore.

At first, no one had realized that there was anything wrong, that the mission had brought something back. But then the corpses of the recently dead had begun to move. And not just move, but attack those who were still living. It wasn't long after that, that everything changed. Angela had been only ten years old at the time.

She watched the adults as they buzzed around the apartment. Something was wrong today. Usually everyone was so slow. They walked slow, talked slow, even thought slow. It was how they survived the boredom of days trapped inside the building. Over a month ago, if Angela had the passage of time correct, they had stopped being able to leave the building. So many corpses had gathered around that they couldn't leave. In fact, they couldn't even use the first few floors anymore. Although, like the other children, the only time Angela had ever gone outside since the apartment had become their fort was when she went out on the balconies.

"What's going on?" she asked as Hunter passed by the corner where she was drawing pictures. She liked Hunter. When her mom had suffered a bite, her dad had packed Angela up and moved them away. Her dad was very sick though; he had always been. He didn't have enough medicine, and when he couldn't take care of Angela anymore, he made Hunter promise to. Hunter had found them and helped them not long after leaving home. He saved their lives many times.

"It looks like we're going to be leaving the apartment, sweet pea," Hunter told her.

"How? And where will we be going?"

"We're still working on the how, but I think I have an idea. As for where we're going, do you remember the little old lady on the radio?"

"Of course. She sounds nice."

"Well, she agreed to take us in if we can get there."

"Isn't she far off into the woods?"

"Yes. But as long as we're careful, we can make it."

"If you say so. I haven't heard her in awhile." Angela was annoyed that she couldn't remember exactly how long it had been.

"I do say so. And we haven't heard from her because the batteries in her radio died, but don't worry, we talked to her about this a long time ago. Now, can you gather up your things for me? They want me to go with the first batch of people leaving, and I want you with me. Once you have everything together, I'll help you pack."

"Okay." Angela was scared about leaving the apartment building, but she trusted Hunter. He had protected her so far, and was very good at killing the corpses. It was strange that you could kill a corpse, although you had to smash in its head to do it. Hunter said it had something to do with the brain, that you had to destroy the brain. Thankfully, with Hunter around, Angela had never had to try that.

Angela didn't have much, just a few toys, clothes, and bedding, so it didn't take very long for her to gather her things. Some of the other kids had a lot more because the apartment had been their home before the corpses came.

"Let's see what you have." Hunter knelt before her pile of objects and started going through it. "Well this you'll have to take." He picked up her stuffed bunny, Mr. Foof, and set it aside.

Before the corpses, Angela had been starting to think that having Mr. Foof was babyish, but now she clung to him fiercely as the last toy she owned from home. The only other thing Hunter picked out of the pile was her sleeping bag.

"What about clothes?" Angela asked.

"I think what you're wearing is fine. The old lady apparently has a lot, and she can sew and make you new ones."

"Okay."

"I'm going to fill the rest of your bag with goodies. Can you go find Mrs. Craw? She said she'd braid your hair for you."

Angela left to find Mrs. Craw. She was a nice lady, and she braided Angela's long, auburn hair into a pair of neat pigtails down her back.

"Are you excited to leave?" Mrs. Craw asked.

"Oh yes." Angela had been getting tired of the apartments. "But I'm also scared."

"Don't you worry, dear. The rest of us won't be too far behind you. And Hunter will take good care of you."

"I know. That's why I'm not *too* scared."

"Good girl." Mrs. Craw kissed her forehead like Angela's mom used to do, then sent her back to Hunter.

"Ah, just in time. This bag isn't too heavy for you, is it?" Hunter handed her a beige backpack.

Angela picked up the bag and tested its weight. It was heavier than her school bag used to be on normal days, but not by too much, and she told Hunter so.

"Good. It's full of food and drink. Now, you can eat some of it while we travel, but most of it is for the old lady, okay? So don't go pigging out."

Angela laughed. "I won't."

"I have one last thing for you." Hunter reached behind him and pulled a bright red cloak out of the closet. It was a beautiful cloak. The outside was a waterproof material while the inside was made of a soft red fur. It had a black tassel tie-up and black trim, as well as a large hood.

"What's this for?" Angela asked as Hunter draped it over her shoulders and tied it up. It was really comfy.

"To keep you warm and dry in case it rains." Once the cloak was tied around her, he adjusted the locket around her neck, which held pictures of her parents.

"It's so red," she commented. Not that she didn't like the colour. Angela had always loved the colour red.

"So I'll always be able to spot you easily," Hunter smiled.

Angela smiled back.

 ✤

The first group of people were ready to go. They stood on the roof of the apartment building, about ten stories off the ground. Angela was the only kid going with the first group.

"So how are we getting down?" Angela didn't want to look over the edge of the building. She wasn't scared of heights, but she didn't want to see all the corpses gathered on the streets below.

"Watch." Hunter picked up his big hunting bow. Angela had seen him kill lots of corpses with it. He went over to the door they had come out of and picked up an arrow resting there. There was a thick rope tied to the end of the arrow, while the other end was tied tightly to a metal railing near the door.

"You'll only have one shot," someone else on the roof said.

"And I'll make it." Hunter walked to the edge and affixed a strange contraption to the end of the arrow.

"What's that for?" Angela wondered.

"You know what grappling hooks are? This will turn the arrow into a grappling hook once it passes through something," Hunter explained.

"Just remember that it severely reduces accuracy. As will the rope," Mr. Baker said. Mr. Baker had been some sort of military man. He had all sorts of neat stuff and had probably given the thing attached to the arrow to Hunter.

"I've never missed a shot yet." Hunter put one of his feet on the short wall around the roof and aimed toward a shorter building next door.

Angela watched his strong arms pull back on the bowstring. When he released, the arrow whistled across the gap. It struck an air duct on top of the other building and stuck there.

"Told you I wouldn't miss." Hunter smiled at Mr. Baker.

They retied the rope on their end so that it was tight. Mr. Baker crossed the gap first. He looped a strap over the rope, and by holding both ends, he slid down the rope all the way to other roof.

"I'm scared," Angela told Hunter. "I don't think I'll be able to hold on as well as Mr. Baker."

"You won't have to," Hunter assured her. "You're going to wear this."

He helped her get into a harness that strapped around her legs and waist. Mr. Baker secured the rope better on the other building and another man went across.

"Our turn."

"We're going together?" Angela was afraid to go alone.

"Of course." Hunter attached her harness to the rope. He then looped a belt over it, which he wrapped around his arms. His bow and arrows sat strapped to his back alongside a big hiker's bag. He also had a hatchet hanging off his belt. "You ready?"

Angela wasn't, but she nodded anyway.

"Hold on to me."

Angela wrapped her arms around Hunter, and he pushed them both off the roof. They whizzed across the open air, with nothing beneath them but the corpses. At the other end, Mr. Baker caught them before they could hit into anything. Angela was quickly helped out of her harness.

"Was that fun?" Hunter asked, sounding a little breathless and smiling ear to ear.

"A little." Angela hadn't thought it was fun at all, but she wanted to be brave for Hunter.

When the other three people had crossed, they were ready to get off the building. They climbed down a fire escape on the far side, leaving the rope to span the buildings for those who would be coming later.

On the street, Angela felt the old fear. The old fear she had had when she first left home with her dad all that time ago. The fear of uncertainty, of the unknown.

The first time she had ever felt that fear was when she had been a very small girl and became convinced that a werewolf was living in her closet and a witch lived under her bed. That was when she had been given Mr. Foof, to scare away those fictional monsters. Unfortunately the corpses weren't fictional, and so Mr. Foof had no real power over them.

As they moved through the street, Mr. Baker led the way. Angela was kept in the middle of the group, with Hunter right beside her. They were heading for the woods, but first they had to reach the edge of town.

Then the corpses found them.

Mr. Baker turned a corner, only to stumble backwards. A swarm of corpses poured out after him. Hunter grabbed Angela and started running another way. Hunter was strong. He ran quickly, despite the weight of Angela and her bag added to his own gear. Angela buried her face in his shoulder, not wanting to see what was happening to Mr. Baker, or the others, or to see if the corpses were chasing them. As long as Hunter was running fast, they should be safe.

Corpses were slow things. They could be very quiet, and were completely relentless, but they were slow. Just so long as Hunter didn't make a wrong turn like Mr. Baker had, they would be safe.

სა

Once they reached the edge of the woods, Hunter found the path they were supposed to follow. According to the old lady, if they followed it, they would reach her cabin.

"Why does she live in a cabin?" Angela wondered for the first time.

"She said it was her husband's hunting lodge. She went there when the corpses came because it's remote."

"It must be lonely for her to be living there all by herself."

"I'm sure it is. That's probably why she was always talking to us over the radio, and why she so readily agreed to let us come."

"I liked it when she read stories to us. She reminded me of my Grandma then."

"Mine too." Hunter laughed.

It was just the two of them in the woods. When Mr. Baker was attacked, they got separated from the others. Hunter said everything would be okay though. He said that they all knew where the path was and that they could all find their way to the grandmotherly lady's house.

As they walked through the woods, Angela held Hunter's hand. When he suddenly squeezed it, she stopped walking and looked up at him. Hunter was listening to something, but Angela couldn't hear what. He looked worried, which worried Angela. Slowly he knelt down to whisper to her.

"I need you to do something for me." He was being very serious.

"What?" Angela whispered back.

"I need you to follow the path by yourself."

"Why?"

"There's a horde coming down the path behind us. Corpses."

Angela trembled. "I can't."

"You can. You're a big girl, and you're very brave. I know you can do this."

"What are you going to do?"

"I'm going to lead them away."

"No."

"It's okay. It'll be just like that time I told you to hide in the closest of that house, remember? I led the corpses away, and then I came back for you."

"I remember. You'll come back this time, right?"

"Right. But I need you to keep walking down the path. Can you do that for me? I promise I'll find you. How could I possibly miss something this red?" He smiled and pulled her hood up onto her head.

Angela nodded.

"Good girl." Hunter gave her a big hug, then got up and stepped into the trees. He watched and waited for Angela to get moving, so she started walking down the path. The large hood made it difficult to look back over her shoulder for him, but she didn't dare take it off. She would keep her cloak on forever if it would bring Hunter back.

❦

Walking through the woods alone was spooky. Angela kept thinking she heard things in the trees, but when she looked, there was never anything there. She would keep going though, and be brave for Hunter. She tried to imagine that it was him making those noises, as he followed her through the forest. She knew he could travel without being seen or heard when he wanted to.

A great rustling came from the bushes ahead of her. Angela froze. From her belt, she pulled out a small knife that Hunter had given her a long time ago. It wasn't very big, not much fiercer than a letter opener really, but she had been told it could kill a corpse if driven through its eye. She would have to be very close to do that though. She was told to run from corpses, but she was afraid she would lose the path if she did that.

The rustling got closer and closer to the path ahead of Angela. She thought about hiding somewhere, but didn't know if any of the trees nearby were large enough. Besides, she couldn't walk silently through the dead leaves like Hunter could.

It wasn't a corpse that came through the trees. It was a dog, a big, black one that might have been some sort of husky, or shepherd. Angela looked at the dog, frightened, not knowing if it was feral. The dog stood its ground, blocking the path, sniffing at Angela. Slowly, the girl took a step toward it. The dog lowered its head, but kept its ears turned toward Angela. Angela knew that if the dog flattened its ears, then it was angry and she should keep her distance.

"It's okay," she whispered. "I'm not going to hurt you."

The dog raised its head and trotted right up to Angela. She held out her hand and let the big mutt sniff her. When he seemed to accept her, she started to stroke him. She found a dirty collar matted into his fur. Although the tags were missing, the collar had the word Wolf stitched into it.

"Is your name Wolf?" Angela rubbed her hands over his ears. The dog's tail swished back and forth. "Well even if it's not, I'm going to call you Wolf."

Angela started to walk down the path again. Wolf followed along after her.

Travelling with Wolf wasn't nearly as scary as travelling alone. In fact, Angela even started to sing a bit. She sang a song her mother had taught about travelling through the woods to see Grandma, which seemed like a very fitting song. She sang very quietly, however, just in case Wolf wasn't the only thing in the forest.

She wished Wolf could talk. She talked to him about things, like the apartment building and Hunter, but she wished that he could talk back. It would be less lonely if he could talk back.

As she sang her song for the seventh time, Wolf suddenly grabbed the hem of her red cloak.

"Wolf," she hissed at him. "No. Bad."

Wolf kept tugging. He was trying to pull her toward a much smaller and overgrown path to one side.

"We're supposed to go this way," Angela told him. "Hunter said we have to follow the path."

Wolf was very insistent. Every time Angela moved toward him to slacken the cloak, he would back further down the small path and tug it again.

A loud and eerie groan came from the woods up ahead. Angela's blood went cold, for she knew that was the sound of a corpse. Wolf must have smelled it, and was trying to get Angela to avoid it. Corpses always smelled really bad.

"Okay, Wolf." Angela headed down the tiny path. "Hunter didn't say there would be any branches, but maybe this is the way we're supposed to go."

Once Wolf saw that Angela was walking down the path he wanted her to follow, he stopped pulling on the lovely red cloak. Angela wrapped the cloak more tightly around herself, her backpack making a bulge beneath it.

She didn't know how much time had passed, and thought that maybe she should stop for lunch. She wasn't hungry, however. Even though she didn't need to worry about running out of food with her backpack being so full, she was afraid that the corpse on the bigger path would find her if she stopped. She also recalled Hunter saying that the food was for the old lady. Angela didn't know how much food she had, and didn't want to eat any in case the old lady really needed it. Instead, she just kept walking, with Wolf leading the way, hoping that Hunter would find her soon.

꿏

It was a long time later, when the sky had turned pink from the setting sun, and Angela's feet felt like they were going to fall off, that she found the cabin. She assumed it must be the old lady's cabin because she didn't know who else it could possibly belong to.

Relieved by the sight of it, Angela slipped her aching arms out of her backpack. She and Wolf walked up to the cabin door, where Angela politely knocked. She realized she didn't know the old woman's name.

"Grandmother!" she called through the door, hoping that it would do. "Please let me in. I've walked such a long way."

There was no answer. Angela rested her bag next to the door and tried the handle. It was unlocked.

"Hello?" she called as she gently pushed the door open.

Wolf tried to get in too, but Angela wouldn't let him. She slipped into the house and closed the door on the dog's face. Angela didn't know how the old lady felt about dogs, and didn't feel right just inviting him in.

"Grandmother lady?" Angela said to the empty cabin.

It was a big cabin made of wood, decorated fancily with nice furniture, and had antlers mounted over the fireplace. It had high ceilings with exposed crossbeams. Angela thought it was a lovely place, and perfectly matched the voice she had heard over the radio. And she saw a radio in the corner, which Angela took to mean she was in the right place. She liked it a lot better than the apartment building.

She found a door in one wall and opened it. It led into a bedroom. On the bed, was the shape of a person sleeping beneath the blankets, her back to the door. The old lady was asleep, that's why she hadn't heard Angela. Quietly, Angela walked up to the bed.

"Grandmother?" she said, wanting to wake her gently. She reached out and carefully shook the woman's shoulder. When she did, a most fowl stench came from her. "Grandmother, what is that smell?" She took a step back, repulsed.

The old lady suddenly sat up, turning to face Angela. Her eyes were milky white. Her lips pulled back over yellowing teeth. Her skin sagged more than an old woman's normally would, and it was so pale.

The woman was a corpse.

Angela gasped and backed away. She bumped into the doorframe, stumbled, and fell onto her back into the living room. The corpse got out of the bed and moved on unsteady legs toward the fallen girl. Angela screamed and crawled backward, crab-like, her cloak dragging along the floor beneath her. The old woman's corpse reached the girl and fell upon her.

The corpse's eyes were large, nearly bulging out of her head at Angela. Her large nose had already begun to rot, taking on a blackish tone. The grandmotherly lady's mouth was by far the worst. It stretched wide open, large and dark and full of death.

Angela managed to protect her face. She grabbed the corpse's shoulders and held it back, while its teeth gnashed and bit just inches away from her nose. Angela kept screaming. She could hear Wolf outside, barking his head off near one of the windows. He couldn't get in though. And Angela couldn't reach her little knife on her belt, as she had to use all her strength to hold back the corpse. The corpse's hands were clawing at her shoulders, but the cloak was managing to protect them from harm.

"Angela!" a mighty voice screamed from outside.

The door smashed open. The running of heavy boots boomed across the floor. Angela watched as a hatchet buried itself deep into the side of the corpse's head, knocking it sideways and off her.

"Angela, are you all right?" It was Hunter, and he swept the girl up off the floor and into his arms.

"I didn't think you'd find me. I took a different path," she sobbed into his chest.

"I told you I would find you. I will always find you my little sweet pea. My little red."

Wolf whined from nearby. Angela looked up and saw the dog sitting next to them.

"A friend of yours?" Hunter asked.

"Yes." Angela patted Wolf's head. "His name is Wolf."

"Well how about you, me, and Wolf get out of here. It's not as safe here as we thought and we kind of made a lot of noise."

"Okay." Angela managed to let go of Hunter and get to her feet. Holding hands, they left the cabin, picking up her bag by the door as they went.

Wolf led them into the woods, knowing which way was best to avoid more corpses.

"Hunter? Can you carry me? My feet hurt."

"Sure thing." Hunter scooped her up into his big arms.

"And Hunter?"

"Yes?"

"Will we ever get to live happily ever after?"

"One day. I promise."

❧

Kristal Stittle *was born and raised in Toronto, Canada, where she still lives with her cat. She writes prolifically during her free time, whether it be novels, scripts, or short stories. She also paints and illustrates regularly.*

She Sleeps

Vivian Caethe

The comet sang across the sky in colors of blue and red, shimmering like the brightest star in the sky. We were running out of ammo at the front door to the castle at the end of the world. The old-style castle was nestled into the side of a mountain in the Ozarks, the last bastion of the secretive government program known only as Briarthorn.

The horde of *shoggoths* slavered up the hill at us as I emptied the clip of my Glock .45 into a succession of cult leaders. If you got the smart ones fast enough, the rest would just mill around for a while, easy pickings. Although this time, my hard-won strategy was not working as well as I had hoped. They just kept on coming. The ones in the back, the leaders with the books, chanted as the ones toward the front rushed at us, dark magics crackling at their fingertips.

"Cover me!" I shouted.

Next to me, Marcus let loose a series of short bursts with his automatic conversion AK-47. Dark ichor splattered the pavement at our feet as I reloaded. Ammo was getting harder to come by these days. If we failed in our mission, we might as well use the rest of it to go out in a blaze of glory. I risked a glance back at our destination. If we could get past the front gates of the government compound, we could get in and secure the facility.

I aimed and fired, killing the last cult leader. As it fell, the cohesion of the *shoggoths* crumbled, the disconnected underlings losing the organizing effect of the leaders. Marcus and Hoffaker laid down a spray of bullets to discourage any further involvement from the horde as I dashed to the security gate to input the code.

Even months into the invasion, the generators had kept the facility going. They wouldn't last much longer, though. There would be no second chance to access the gateway. The cultists were growing stronger every day. And if the generators failed, the support systems they had hooked the gateway to would fail as well. The prophecy stated that she was the only thing keeping the gateway stable. If she died, the experts told us, the connection to the other planes would lock open.

The local government what remained of it, had organized the best of the best, namely yours truly and some other guys, to awaken Briar Rose.

The name had come up when we did the briefing.

Her bio and photo had been in the information packet they'd handed out, printed on paper that was quickly becoming scarce. She had been at the epicenter of the invasion, when they had poured out of the earth to take over the world. No one was sure why, but the specialists had predicted that if we could get to her, we could close the gateway they had opened into our reality. And maybe if we stopped the flow of unnamable horrors, we could finally turn the war.

The ops pics we had of her gave her the name. She slept on a bier at the center of the high, ceremonial chamber, her long blond hair undone from her braid, her desert camouflage BDUs accentuating her figure. We didn't know what had happened to the rest of her team, or where they had gone. The images had been taken by remote robot after the first three missions sent in after her had not come back. None of the photos from the robot had spoken of their fate. Or whether they had even made it to the chamber where she laid.

The squints theorized that what kept her sleeping was also what kept the gateway open. If we could get past the wall of thorns, the euphemistically titled security structure, and into the inner chamber, we might have a chance to save the world. Which was why I was bashing combinations of numbers into a recalcitrant keypad.

Marcus backed into me and yelled, deaf from the gunfire. "Taking your time there, Prince Charming?"

"Shut up." I gritted my teeth and tried the combination again. I didn't know why I had gotten stuck with the nickname. They all thought it was hilarious though. Maybe it was that I had been the first to comment that Briar Rose wasn't too bad looking. Either way, it was annoying.

Irritated, I tried the combination a third time, my fingers mashing the buttons. The gate opened with a thunk of locks unlatching. I let out the breath I didn't know I'd been holding.

The eight of us hustled through the gate and I slammed it behind us. The horde of cultists and *shoggoths* broke like a moaning wave against the chain-link fencing. Groaning against the weight of corrupted humanity and unthinkable abominations, the flimsy fencing barely kept them back as we rapidly made our way to the next security checkpoint.

This one was more robust and required both a manual key and a biometric reader. They'd promised me that they'd have my information remotely hacked into the system by our ETA to the facility, but that was no guarantee that they had actually been able to make it work. I fished the key out of the pocket of my bulletproof vest and jammed it into the lock. The key resisted my efforts and for one horrified second, I thought they'd given me the wrong key.

The chain link fence crumpled and I heard Marcus swear. "They've got another leader. Damn cultists are responding faster than we can shoot 'em down."

"We have incoming." Hoffaker drawled, spitting a gob of chewing tobacco. "You wanna step it up there, your highness?"

I tried the key again. This time it turned and I smashed my hand against the handprint reader. "Moment of truth, boys."

The damned machine took its own sweet time recognizing my handprint. Long enough that I started to wonder if it was going to get around to doing it at all. Behind me, Jerry let loose a string of expletives as he took out the most recent cult leader. The locks clicked and the gate slowly opened. After we were all inside, I slammed the emergency button with one hand while I took out another cult leader.

If we could destroy the book all the leaders had a copy of, then maybe we'd have a chance to keep them down permanently.

The gate closed with aching slowness and I gritted my teeth as I fired off nine more rounds. One cultist after another fell. Boom, headshot.

Finally snapping closed, the heavy gate took off several appendages from the oozing *shoggoths*. They lay twitching on the ground with the energy of whatever kept them going. In the relative peace that followed, we double timed it across the lawn to the facility.

The top secret complex was silent as we approached it. In the moonlight, I looked at the map the squints had drawn us. Even with the helpful proliferation of detail, it was difficult to navigate through the labyrinth of buildings to the pinnacle. Briar Rose would be in the highest building, in the highest floor. There were unknown hazards between us and her. We had entered no man's land.

We had to get there before the comet aligned with the top of the castle. Glancing up, I saw that it was rapidly crossing the sky, as the prophecy had foretold. I don't know where the squints had gotten their hands on one of the cult leaders' books, but they'd only been able to translate some of it. It said that the woman would be the key and that the gates would fully open when the comet kissed her face.

The image on her photo flashed through my mind. Maybe part of the reason why I wanted to save her from that fate was that she looked like my wife. I hadn't been able to save Mary from death at the hands of the cultists, but I would be damned if I'd let them take another woman.

"Why'd you think there's no cultists in here?" Jerry asked nervously. "Surely there were employees here when they accidentally activated the artifact."

"Bet they killed them all in the cover up, before things got really bad. They should have known better thought." Doc's conspiracy theories were showing again.

"Be quiet." I stopped and tilted my head. "You boys hear that?"

"Hear what?" Inevitably, Freddy spoke up just as I thought I heard the sound again.

"It sounds like… singing." Danver frowned. "I thought there wasn't supposed to be anyone in here."

"There's not." I reloaded my Glock and gestured with my chin up to the building at the top of the stairway up the mountain. "It's coming from her building."

"Crap." Wilson was the religious type, for him that was the foulest curse word imaginable.

"Yeah. Crap." I nodded at Marcus. He and I took the lead as we scurried up the stairway to our objective.

The singing came faintly down the curving staircase, the sound echoing eerily to the tune of the chanting cultists in the distance. I wondered for a moment if she was singing.

We reached the front door of the castle without seeing any signs of life. I traded glances with Marcus and reached into my pocket for the prox key. Swiping the key against the reader, I took a deep breath. "Here we go."

I pushed open the door as Marcus covered me, nearly gagging at the stench that billowed out. Rotten flesh and ammonia with a hint of garlic. The smell of *shoggoths*.

No one knew where the *shoggoths* had come from. Or why they seemed to follow the commands of the cult leaders. I sure as hell couldn't explain it. But I knew 'em when I smelled 'em.

"Crap crap crap crap crap." Wilson had developed a tic.

I tried to breathe shallowly as I led the way into the building. The crooning song grew louder, coming from one of the hallways that led off from the main lobby. I glanced around warily, taking in the normal looking lobby. The entire place had been converted to office-style monotony. There was even a fake potted plant. It had been used as a R&D facility for so long that it had lost whatever charm had been imbued in it by its previous owners.

Catching the door before it banged into the wall, I gestured the others through. Doc came last and gave me a knowing nod. Of all of us, he was the conspiracy theorist. I knew he was already cooking up some explanation of why there were *shoggoths* in the secure research facility lab. I sniffed. There had to be at least three of them. As crackbrained as the answer would be coming from Doc, the question was still valid. Why were they here?

Before I had time to ponder the matter further, one of them came down the hallway at us, screeching with as it shifted to a vaguely humanoid form. Jerry shot it in the head, a clean hit straight in the forehead, but it absorbed the blow and kept on coming.

"What the hell?" Hoffaker yelled. He raised his pistol, but it was too fast, on him before any of us could act. It bit down on his arm, tearing away a chunk of flesh. Marcus opened fire, riddling Hoffaker and the shoggoth with bullets. They fell in a horrible embrace, twitching on the floor, drying a final death as they bled out, red blood and black ichor. The smell intensified.

"All right, new plan." I said as Marcus reloaded. "The people with the big guns go first."

Marcus nodded as Doc crouched to relieve Hoffaker of his Smith and Wesson. I went to the side of the door where the fire plan for the building was helpfully posted. "All right, she should be on the fourth floor in the tower. We have an unknown number of *shoggoths* and cultists between here and there, with probable cult leaders as well. This means close quarters combat with stronger *shoggoths* than normal. Marcus and I will go first. Doc, you take the rear. Any questions?"

There were no questions.

Marcus and I edged forward into the hallway, the others behind us covering the corners. The rest of the first floor was clear, but that only worried me more as the smell of the *shoggoths* intensified. The stairwell up was also clear, but there were strange stains on the walls and ceilings, as if something was oozing down from the higher floors.

The first floor stairwell was clear, and when we reached the second floor, we paused to listen. The only sound in the building was our harsh breathing in the close quarters of the stairwell. Cautiously, we proceeded upwards.

We kept our silence as we reached the fourth floor door. I swiped the prox key over the reader and winced when it beeped loudly. Pausing to listen, I heard nothing. The singing had stopped.

Easing the door open, I peered through the crack. The walls of the fourth level were caked with green-black ooze that shimmered like an oil slick under the fluorescent lights. The floor was clear. "Don't touch the walls."

We made an uneasy procession through the door into the floor. Marcus covered me as I peered around the corner toward the chamber where they kept Briar Rose. "Seems clear. Let's go."

Creeping up the hall, we cleared each room that we passed before moving on. Nothing makes a bad day worse than a cultist or a shoggoth coming up behind you. Especially with how fast they were moving.

We passed five doors until we came to the door of her chamber. "Moment of truth, gentlemen."

Marcus crouched next to me as I swiped the prox key. The beep was alarm-loud in the silence we had only broken by the sound of our breathing. A screech followed and an immense shoggoth yanked the door off its hinges. The sound of the singing started again, deafening us with its eerie intensity.

Marcus riddled the shoggoth with bullets before I could stop him. I could see the bier past the twitching shoggoth; Marcus had only barely missed her.

The *shoggoths* attacked all at once, none of the nice one after another like you see in the movies. Our only saving grace was the narrow door. We retreated several feet as they bottlenecked. As one, we opened fire, aiming for headshots in the vain hope that they would fall. They kept coming.

The stuttering gunfire lost a harmony as Marcus ran out of ammunition. Dropping the AK he pulled his Colt M1911 and kept firing. I emptied one clip, ejected it, and slapped another one in.

There were seven of them and the three at the front took the brunt of the fire. They fell, twitching toward us as the manic glare in their inhuman eyes slowly went out. The four behind considered the situation. They poured out at us one at a time, impossibly fast.

We hit the first with the rest of our ammo. I barely had time to reload before one of them was on me. Impossibly sharp teeth latched onto my Kevlar undershirt, trying to find purchase as the material barely protected my arm. Turning my head away, I placed my Glock against the side of its head and fired. Once. Twice. Three times. Its skull shattered.

Kicking the oozing corpse away from me, I turned to find three of our men down. Marcus fought hand to hand with one of the *shoggoths*. His Colt lay on the ground, the slide open, empty. I reloaded as I ran to him. Point blank, I fired, keeping him out of the crossfire. One. Two. Three.

Shoggoth splattered everywhere, coating Marcus' face and clothes. I was already covered with it. There weren't enough showers in the world.

The others weren't doing as well. Jerry was already down. The sixth shoggoth chewed at his face, crunching and slurping. Danver and Freddy were lying face down in a puddle of goo, not moving. Leaning against the wall, Doc was moaning, his eyes already starting to glaze over. I sighed; we needed him to figure out how to wake Briar Rose. "Hell."

My count was off. The last shoggoth dropped from the ceiling like a spider, landing on my back. I fell to one knee and rolled, trying to shake it off. Realizing what it was after, I barely got my arm between its teeth and my spine. It clamped down on the much-abused Kevlar; I could feel its teeth through the material, strong as a vise.

To my horror, I felt the tendrils of the song insinuating themselves in my mind. I found myself relaxing, my arm dropping from its teeth as the crooning song wended its way through my thoughts. It was so beautiful.

She was so beautiful.

The sound of gunfire close to my ear broke the spell and the shog-goth screeched. Deafened, I toppled, the shoggoth still on top of me.

Shaking myself free, I rolled. From a prone position, I emptied the last six shots into the creature. Its body shook with the impacts.

My ears ringing, I accepted Marcus' hand up and stood on shaky legs.

He said something, but I shook my head, pointing at my ears. He raised his voice. "You ok?"

Nodding, I reloaded, taking no chances this time. The *shoggoths* were in here for a reason. It didn't matter how they got in here, but it was possible our objective had been compromised. The singing had stopped at some point, or maybe my ears were just ringing too loudly.

We stepped around bodies and piles of goo to Doc. I waited until Marcus shot him in the head. The last thing we needed was another monster at our backs. After I was sure he was dead, I fished through his vest pockets for the small medical kit. We'd wake her up and get the hell out of here. If we could make it to the field behind the complex, the helo could pick us up. I checked my watch. The last flight of carefully hoarded fuel was due in fifteen minutes.

Briar Rose lay on her bier like a fairy tale princess. In person she was prettier than I expected, a tangle of golden hair framing her perfect features. Even though her body was painfully thin, she was the sort of girl I would have dreamed of dating in college.

Glancing at Marcus, I saw him take up a sentry position at the door. Reassured, I unpacked the medical draw kit and tried to remember the EMT lessons I had learned in the military. It was close to ten years ago. God, I felt old.

The first step was to get her blood pressure and check her vitals. The next step was to get a blood sample for the squints. Then at some point I would figure out how to wake her up. That part of the plan was hazy. I don't think they actually expected us to get this far.

I checked her pulse, feeling the beat beneath my fingers. Glancing out the window, I saw the comet approaching closer, growing brighter in the sky. Her heartbeat sped up to meet it.

Vitals, check. The blood sample was next. As the needle pierced her veins, she sucked in a breath and opened her eyes. I looked into the dark pools of her eyes. I heard her voice in my head.

Hello dear prince.

The needle dropped from my nerveless fingers as I lost myself in her eyes. I felt, rather than saw, her smile as I leaned close to kiss her. Her sharp teeth bit into my lip and I felt the song of the unknown depths sing through my veins. I heard the comet's light touch the window of her chamber.

The universe screamed her name.

Vivian Caethe's *short stories and novellas have appeared in a variety of magazines and anthologies. Her most recent novella,* The Diamond City, *is published by* Bold Strokes Books. *While writing, thinking and breathing in general, she drinks tea in the constant search for the perfect cup. She lives in Colorado with her husband, a dog who thinks he's a human with hyper-trichosis, and a supervillan cat.*

LILITH'S MIRROR

Anne Bean

For many years I have waited patiently in my cave, darkness like a womb. Silent, I wait to be born. I watch the window into the Other World, its surface silver and shimmering. I can see very little: unpainted wooden walls, an old oak chest of drawers, a stool, and plenty of dust. I can hear distant hushed voices, the screaming of a newborn child, the strangled cry of the mother, and then the voice of the father wailing out kaddish. Suddenly, someone covers my mirror in a cloth, rich damask that blocks out the light. I can still hear: the voice of another woman, a nervous voice that whispers in the dark, *Surely I am the fairest. Surely he will have eyes for none but me*. She is the one who will find me, I am sure of it. She will set me free.

The day comes when the cloth is drawn back, light floods my cave, and I can see the woman who will be my deliverance. She looks young, more than a girl but less than a woman. She has curly black hair, round breasts pushed up by overzealous corsetry, red lips, and creamy white skin. Her young body looks so delicious; I want to eat her all up.

She gazes at her face and body in the window to my cave. She does not see me, of course. She sees only herself, and I watch as she examines a spot on her nose, strokes her neck to ensure that her skin is smooth. She strides away to snatch a pot of cream off the vanity, and applies it to her face. When she leaves, she covers up the mirror again with the cloth, and I am once again bathed in darkness.

But, I am patient.

Soon enough, she'll say the spell. And then she'll be mine.

Some days she looks into the mirror for just a few moments, fixing a stray hair or painting her lips red as blood. Other days she spends more time, staring for long minutes into her own face, or even disrobing and touching each part of her body in turn, checking for any blemish or mark that would mar her milk-white skin. I feel heat grow inside me when she fingers each rib, each nipple. I can see the buzzing hive of worry inside her mind: the women in the village talking in whispers and giggles, staring at her husband when they think she isn't looking.

I must be the fairest, she whispers on the days when she stands naked before me. *He must be only mine.*

And then one day, when she's thinking about the glance her husband had given the fleshy rump of the butcher's wife, she says the words. *Mirror, mirror, on the wall, who's the fairest of them all?*

I let out a sigh of pure pleasure, and she stiffens. She can hear me now. A tiny piece of myself is inside her already. *Though many beauties be in the land, my Queen*, I whisper, *Thou art the fairest to be seen*. She gasps and throws the cloth hurriedly over the mirror, but I am not concerned. She'll be back.

Two days later, she returns. She's wearing a rich red gown and her hair hangs down to her waist. She glances around the room to ensure that she's alone and then whispers to me, *Mirror, mirror on the wall, who's the fairest of them all?* And like clockwork, I reply. *Though many beauties be in the land, O Queen, thou art the fairest to be seen*. And somewhere in the distance I hear the laughter of a little girl. The woman purses her lips and throws the cloth back over the portal between us. In the darkness, I smile. The step-child, of course. Now I know how I will birth myself into this world.

I am ever so patient. I wait until the laughter of the child has turned into the piping questions of a girl have turned into the songs and prayers of a young woman. All the while the stepmother, my vessel, comes to me. She is older now, applying cream fervently to the corners of her eyes. I see the image of her stepdaughter growing in her mind and I know that she is a beautiful child. The day I hear the distant prayers of the Bat Mitzvah is the day I strike.

The woman comes to me with eyes red from tears. She disrobes and performs her ritual check of body parts. She finds flaws with her neck, as usual. My anticipation fills me with a delicious warm ache. She takes a breath, finally, and says it. *Mirror, mirror on the wall, who's the fairest of them all?* And I watch her face crumble as I speak: *While your beauty, my Queen, is ever so rare, there is one who has a face more fair*. Her

whole body twists as if in pain. She bites her lip to keep from screaming. *Who?* she whispers, and grips the edge of the frame. *Who is he
looking at now?*

And I send the image to grow inside her mind like a cancer: Her
stepdaughter, laughing with her friends in the afternoon sunlight,
long black hair, snow-white skin, lips red from sneaking in to use her
stepmother's makeup. Her husband, sitting some distance away, a
book open on his lap, staring at the beauty of his daughter, thinking of
how she looks so like her mother.

It is a lie, of course, but a lie infused with enough truth to make the
woman dig her nails into her palms and hiss at me: *IS IT HER?*

And dropping the poetry, I speak the most powerful spell of all: *Yes.
Oh, yes.*

And then she crumbles onto the floor, weeping, her worst fears realized in the confines of her tiny mind. She is open to me now that she is
utterly broken. I flood into the shell that is left of her, flow into her red
round mouth and her green eyes and through her still round and lush
breasts, through her arms and legs until I have even filled her fingers
and toes. And whatever was left of her has flowed backwards, into the
mirror, into the cave.

I feel the vital energy of this body flowing into me. I stretch and perform her ritual touching of parts. And I know she is trapped inside the
mirror, watching me touch her flesh. At last, I put on her clothes, cover
the mirror with the cloth, and walk out of the room.

I find the rest of the family downstairs, tired from the celebrations of
the girl's supposed womanhood. The man is uglier in reality than he
was in the woman's imagination. The girl is lovely enough with dark
hair and smooth pale skin, but she has an overbite that makes her look
a bit like a rabbit. She's called, I have gathered, Beylke, meaning
White. It is a good name for her; she is bland and dull. The family's
wealth, though, is apparent from the rich ornaments around the room
and the girl's dress of fine silk.

"Come," I tell the girl, who looks up at me with animal fear in her
eyes, "embrace your dear mother." She reluctantly stands and ap-
proaches me, puts her arms around my waist. I let my hand fall like a
dead thing on the back of her neck.

"How proud you must be, Beylke," I murmur in the stepmother's
voice, "to finally be a woman."

The man follows his daughter with his eyes. I look into his head and
smile at the irony. He is indeed seeing his dead wife, longing for her
cold bones when they were once warm with flesh. And here I thought

I was making his lustful gaze up as a trick. How well he has followed along. He will make a good dog.

The girl, on the other hand, will be a problem. On the second day I catch her watching her father and me have sex. On the third day, I find the things on my dressing table have been shifted around when I come back from my bath. The girl suspects something. And even if no one would believe the words of a thirteen-year-old girl, what about later? When she becomes a woman? Suppose she learns the truth behind her wicked stepmother and breaks the mirror? My soul would be sucked back into the cave. It must be she, not I, who dies shrieking.

A week later, I find my solution. There is a man who works in the woods, catching rabbits and hunting deer. I have seen how he skins a living creature in one swift pull. One day I walk past his cottage carrying some shopping, wearing my red dress. He is chopping firewood in the yard, muscles bulging against his shirt.

"Pardon me," I say, and he pauses in his chopping. "I have walked from the village, and I am so tired. Might I get a drink of water from your well?"

He looks me up and down, like he might look at a hind to see how much meat he could get out of her. I smile.

"All right," he says, and walks behind the house to draw up a bucket of water. I follow him on silent feet and set the shopping down at the corner of the house. He is busy drawing water, and I tug at the laces of my corset. When he turns around I am standing, naked, lips and legs parted. He looks at me with bewilderment.

"No one will know," I say. The huntsman stares at me, sets down the bucket of water, and folds his arms.

"My husband's seed does not grow," I say. "How do you think he has one daughter from the other wife, and yet none with me? That child is not of his seed. They say her mother bore her by witchcraft, blood magic."

"And you wanted something easy," he says with a smirk.

"That's right," I say. "Easy."

He pushes me against the plank wall of the house and doesn't even take his trousers all the way down. He heaves into me, grunting, like a wild pig. His breath is hot and foul on my neck. I can feel my back chafing on the rough wooden wall. When he's finished, I walk to the well and pour the water he has drawn over my naked body in a great gushing cascade. He watches, still panting.

"You must do one more thing for me," I tell him.

Part of my influence has come into him during our union. He is subdued now, a wild horse broken. "What must I do?"

"You must take my stepdaughter into the woods and kill her."

He nods. He would have done that, I think, even without the sex.

"Then you must cut out her heart and tongue and bring them to me as proof. Will you do this for me?"

He nods. "I will."

I put on my dress. I pick up my shopping. I walk home.

The next day, as my stepdaughter comes skipping home from school, I grab her arm and pull her aside.

"My little snowdrop," I say through teeth clenched in something like a smile, "won't you be so kind as to walk into the woods and pick some flowers for the house?"

She narrows her little blue eyes at me for a moment, then says, "Of course, Stepmother."

"Of course you must call me Mother," I snap, gripping her arm a bit tighter than I intended.

She lowers her eyes. "Yes, Mother." Then she is walking down the path in her little white dress, and I can see the shadow of the huntsman moving in her wake.

When she does not return at sunset, her father begins to fret. *What if she's lost? Where could she be?* At dinner I feed the oaf too much wine, so that he is soon snoring the big bed. I stay up with a candle, waiting. At midnight the huntsman pads up to the back door carrying a little burlap bag moist with blood. I take it into the kitchen, produce the eyes and heart, and put them on a china plate. I don't bother with a knife and fork. I eat them raw; the eyeballs pop in my mouth like grapes.

For weeks I think nothing of her, even while my husband weeps over the disappearance and presumed death of his only child. I wear black, but in my heart I am filled with bliss. I spend my days coupling with the huntsman, with my husband when he'll have me, waiting for the seed to begin growing in my womb, the first of my many children. And then, alas, I look in the mirror.

One day I find myself upstairs in the attic room with the mirror, and just on a whim, I twitch aside the cloth. She is still waiting in the darkness. The woman.

What have you done to me? she cries inside my head.

I will have your little life, I reply. *I will fill it with my children.*

Then something odd happens: the woman begins to laugh. *She's still alive, you know, our little stepchild.*

I feel the base of my spine stiffen. *What? How would a speck of filth like you know matters of life and death?*

I can feel her from in here. I can't explain how, but I know she still lives.

I toss the damask back over the mirror and hurry to the edge of the forest. The damn mortal was right; my stepdaughter is alive. I can smell her. A growl builds in the back of my throat. The huntsman has served me ill.

Next day I wait 'til my husband is away and paint my face with candle wax and resin until I look like a wart-covered crone. I throw on the oldest rags in the house and take out a trinket I've been saving: long red satin ribbons bought at last week's fair. Carefully, I write on them a spell that will suck the life out of the girl, and sew the ribbons up into corset laces. Then I follow her scent.

A few miles into the woods I find her. There is an old stone hut, some hermit's hovel. The girl's stench is everywhere. I rap at the door.

"Spend a few pennies on a pretty thing?"

She opens the door a crack and peers out. She looks taller; I cannot tell if she's grown or is merely standing up straight. "I'm not supposed to talk to strangers."

"I'm just a peddler, girl. See these lovely laces?"

Her eyes light up and she opens the door all the way. What a fool. She takes off her corset and threads in the red laces. She slips the corset back on over her head.

"Let me help you tighten them, my dear."

"Snow."

"What's that?"

"I'm called Snow now. I used to be someone else, before I came here."

I bark a short laugh. "You give all strangers your true name?"

She looks afraid then, but it is too late, for I am pulling, one knee in pressing into the small of her back, laces squeezing the breath out of her. She falls to the ground in the doorway, dead.

A week later I walk up to the attic room where the mirror is kept and look upon the woman inside. *What do you make of me now*, I ask her, *now that your Snow White is dead?*

You're a fool, the woman snaps, *if you think her dead.*

I must not scream while my husband is downstairs; I am obliged to bite my finger until it bleeds instead. I stare at the blood welling up by the indentations of my teeth. I will try again tomorrow.

The next day I go back in my disguise as a hag. I bring her a comb on which I have burned the words that cause instant death, cleverly hidden in a fancy pattern of flowers and leaves. I soon stand outside her cottage.

"O lady, come see my wares."

The door remains shut, but her voice comes from behind it. "I'm not opening the door for anyone. My protectors have told me so."

"And who might they be?"

"The seven rabbis who live in this forest."

I frown. That is powerful protection indeed. "There's no need to open the door, dearie. Let me show you my wares through the window. After all, even a girl who stays with rabbi will get married someday, right? Then you'll need a lovely comb for your hair..."

The catch in her voice tells me I've struck the right chord. "I...I suppose I could look out the window..."

And her pale face appears at the glass. She pushes the window open, enchanted by the sight of the beautiful comb.

"Go ahead, try it."

She does, and I hear the thud of her body hit the floor. I go home and eat raw meat for dinner, tearing the flesh with glee. I know my husband looks at me strangely, but I distract him later, in bed.

The next morning I stand naked in front of the mirror.

"Does she still live?" I demand.

"You're no better a murderess than I was," the woman smirks. I want to slap her, but alas I cannot without breaking her prison. Instead I throw the cloth over the mirror. I walk to the edge of the wood and tear at the sod with my fingernails. The girl still lives, curse her! Her protection is too powerful. And I must switch tactics.

When I next show up at her door, I am carrying a whole basket of apples and whistling a lively tune.

"Can I interest my lady in a lovely fresh apple?"

"We've played this game already," comes her voice from inside, "and I am quite finished playing."

"You will take this apple, Snow White. You will eat it." And I pronounce a word of command that, coupled with her true name, impels her to open the door. Her eyes are glazed as she reaches into my basket and takes the shiniest, reddest apple off the top.

"This will bring you great knowledge of good and evil, Snow. Think of yourself as Eve."

Her eyes widen then, pupils growing large. With the bite of apple, she sees everything. She sees me wearing her human stepmother's body like a dress. She sees before I took over, her stepmother's tryst with the mirror, all petty jealousy and hatred. She sees her father's lust for her. A tear rolls down her face. I turn my back and walk away, and wait for her to come to me if she dares. I will fight her on my own ground.

At the four corners of the house I have come to think of as mine, I bury a scroll with my true name, written in my own blood. My husband watches me from the window. He is scared, but knows not to get in my way. I march up the stairs to the little room and rip the cloth off the mirror.

"Now I will end this! I have prepared many potent spells to kill Snow and her guardians."

"You are a fool," says the woman behind the mirror. "They are more powerful than you. They will kill you."

"I am not killed so easily."

Near the dawn she finally comes through the door to her former home, wielding an axe and with all seven rabbis at her heels. The rabbis range from dwarfishly small to towering, all dressed in black and chanting, "Out, Lilith!" I begin to speak the spells to burn them, but the words are not enough. Not when they have named me, not when they have swept into a circle surrounding me. They hold my little flesh body fast and I am silent.

They have a pair of iron shoes. I can see the name of the One Who Cannot Be Named on them, the One who has the power of life and death. The rabbis heat them in the fire and bring them, red-hot, to my feet. Snow herself removes my little leather slippers.

My spine spasms as they wrestle the shoes onto my feet with tongs. I can hear the sizzle of flesh, smell myself burning. The agony of the searing metal on skin is exquisite. They stand me up, and I dance. I dance, enchanted, even when the flesh by my ankles is bubbling with blisters. Snow watches with satisfaction twitching at the corners of her mouth.

"Up the stairs!" she commands, and helpless, I dance up to the mirror room. Snow follows.

Once we reach the mirror she whips off the cloth cover and turns to me. She raises the axe above her head, but she does not aim it at my tortured body. She aims it behind me, at the mirror in the gilt frame.

"A gift for you, Mother," she whispers, just loud enough to hear. I am not sure if she speaks to me or the mortal trapped behind the mirror.

With a great crash, the girl brings the axe down into the surface of the glass. The body I have called home screams as I am sucked back through the silvery portal and cast into the darkness. But here is where my true triumph has come to pass. With all her knowledge of good and evil, Snow has taken her revenge. The stepmother, the woman who invited me into her flesh, is back in her own body. Burning.

Dancing. Shrieking. And the girl, she knew it would happen. I could see it in her eyes.

I do not mind being here, alone in the dark. I am nothing if not patient. A new portal will arise. I will wait until the day when the girl-grown-woman, still white as snow and red as blood, finds a mirror of her own to stand before.

❧

Anne Bean *recently received her MFA from Goddard College in Plainfield, Vermont. She lives in Seattle, where she writes, designs books, and geeks out about fairy tales. You can see evidence of said geeking out at* http://annebean.com.

The Potency of Names

David Turnbull

Being to the rear of the building the glass in the window of the Inquisitor's Office was one of the few in the headquarters of the People's Commissariat that remained intact. The Inquisitor paced anxiously up and down in front of it, his diminutive height positively dwarfed by its uncommon length. His breakfast of bread and water lay uneaten amongst the jumbled chaos of un-filed and un-read reports that littered his desktop.

The Republic had been brought to its knees. The citadel, its last bastion, was being starved into submission. The dreadful weather adding to the ominous portents of impending catastrophe. In the early days of the siege the citizens had panicked and riots had ensued. The great statue of Comrade Eulenspiegel had been toppled and brought crashing down in a pile of rubble as fragmented as the cause would soon become.

Acting on orders from the Assembly the Republican Guard acted swiftly to nip the unrest in the bud, firing volley after indiscriminate volley into the seething pandemonium, until the disorderly delinquent crowds finally dispersed to tend to their wounds and mourn their dead.

In the days that followed the ceaseless snowfall had covered up the blood that stained the gutters and buried the bodies that were piled up on the cobblestones under deep, secretive drifts.

Now the streets were empty and as silent as death itself.

At the height of the riots the Commissariat headquarters had been a particular focus of the people's wrath. It still bore the scars of this short-lived but ferociously venomous spat. On its wide stone steps the Clockwork guards stood motionless in the knee-deep snow. One had been unceremoniously decapitated in the melee. His head had been stolen and smuggled away. In the hollow of his neck the cogs and wheels of his mechanized innards had began to bleed the russet red of rust. Immobilized, with his rifle impotently outstretched, his companion's Looking Glass eyes gazed emptily into the distance.

The Inquisitor paused for a moment before the tall window to watch the plump white snowflakes continuing to fall with a depressingly monotonous persistence. The blizzard had lasted for over a fortnight now and everything as far as the eye could see was being suffocated beneath an all-devouring white blanket.

Across the wide adjoining courtyard, in the building which housed the Ministry of Actual Fact and Certain Reality, icicles as long and as sharp harpoons hung down from the lead guttering that fringed the edges of its snow laden rooftop. Amongst the snowfall billows of thick black smoke were sucked and blown on the bitter polar winds. Enormous piles of paper were being incinerated in over crammed braziers. Statistics and data. Proof and evidence.

Lists of names.

Names with potency about them. Names that had been an obsession amongst the higher echelons the Republic's elite cabal. Names that had been outlawed and proscribed. Names of counter insurgents and Royalist dissidents.

Names that were the subject of *tales*. *Tales* that were considered subversive by decree of Comrade Eulenspiegel and the Commissariat. Names that the Inquisitor himself had been tasked to systematically write out of history.

The architects of the revolution understood how names defined people and gave them status. Perhaps Eulenspiegel himself understood this better than anyone. While everyone else in the post revolutionary world had become known simply as Citizen or Comrade, only Eulenspiegel had his name attached to his title. Only the *tales* of Till Eulenspiegel's extensive pre-revolutionary exploits were permitted to be recounted by the masses. The rest was dismissed as stuff and nonsense.

Now, there was a new name to contend with.

A name with a compelling potency of its own.

The Snow Queen had returned from exile to lay claim to the lands so recently liberated from the yoke of the monarchy's oppression. Her advancing expeditionary forces had laid waste of most of the Marchen and had driven the courageous Republican Guard back inside the fortifications of the Citadel. Although valiant in their defiance they were battle weary and depleted in the number and the Inquisitor knew that it would not be long now till the very last remnant of the glorious revolution was swept away.

Demoralizing reports from spies and field agents had been flooding into the headquarters for days. Counter-insurgents and guerrilla fighters were coming down from the mountains to pledge their support to the Queen's cause. To the south the royalist regiments commanded by the Grand Old Duke had reputedly breached the defensive border wall. It was reported that that in the north the six soldiers of fortune, with their various magical gifts, had finally come out of hiding and were heading towards the citadel on seven league boots.

How much of this was fact and how much was subversive counter-revolutionary propaganda was impossible to tell. But the Inquisitor knew without the shadow of a doubt that the end was near. Several key members of the assembly were flat out on the cold slab of the mortuary, others had already fled.

For his part the Inquisitor had a few loose end to tie up. Then he would simply slip away and lie low. Just as he had done when the aristocracy was overthrown. Now, as then, when he judged that the time was right, he would offer his services and his undying loyalty to the new regime. The Queen would be no different in this respect to the Assembly. Whatever their political persuasion those who seized power inevitably required the services of those with the wherewithal and fortitude to do whatever became necessary to ensure they held it tightly within their grip.

Of course he would need a new identity. Another new name. The *People's Inquisitor* was far too closely associated with the Republic. He would disassociate himself with that name and all of the baggage that went with it.

When he presented himself to the Queen he would need a name that fired her imagination and inspired confidence in the potential of his worth to her.

Over the past few days he had been giving the matter some considerable consideration. Toying with the possibilities. The question was not settled. But *Frosty Jack, Jack of the Frost,* or some other permutation on the theme seemed wholly appropriate.

So long as his true name was kept secret and never spoken out loud he had the wherewithal to prosper under any regime. Any assumed name. During his tenure as Inquisitor he had come to appreciate more than ever before the potency of names. Those that he had tortured had drawn power from names. The names given to their *tales*. The names given to their infernal *fetishes* — magic mirrors and tin whistles and tinderboxes. It had become patently obvious to him that the way to diminish them was to destroy the names connected with them. Call them plain citizen. Deny the existence of the *tale*. Call a mirror a mirror and a whistle a whistle and they were nothing.

The irony of the counter effect that his own true name could have on him was something that often taxed him. He did not draw even a gram power from that dreaded name. It was in fact the only weapon that could be used against him to any avail. His Achilles heel. His great weakness. The mere whisper of it could bring about his downfall. The effect on him of hearing it spoken out loud could be devastating.

And so it must never be revealed to anyone.

This was why he felt that the work he had been doing had been so vital. Not in the sense of the trivial political machinations of the Assembly and their misguided credo but the in far more important sense of his own survival. If, as he has almost succeeded in doing, he could suppress all memory of the *tales* he would, in doing so, suppress all memory of his own *tale*. And if no one remembered his *tale* then no one would remember his name. For one was surely the same as the other.

A knock on his door interrupted his thoughts.

The Inquisitor cleared his throat.

"Enter."

The door opened. The Sergeant at Arms appeared, looked down at him, and gave him an officious salute. "The last of the prisoners are being brought out to the yard," he said.

The Inquisitor stroked his narrow moustache and eyed the man absently, not sure for a moment why he was being made aware of this.

"You said that you wished to personally supervise the final executions," the Sergeant at Arms reminded him.

"Ah!" he said. "So I did."

He gave the man a dismissive wave. "Carry on. I will be with you presently."

The Sergeant at Arms straightened his shoulders and raised a clenched fist into the air.

"Long live the revolution!" he said.

"Long live the revolution," joined the Inquisitor.

"Fool!" he spat out loud when the Sergeant closed the door again.

The man obviously still truly believed in all that nonsense about freedom and liberty.

No doubt he would go on believing to his very last breath. Didn't he realize that the revolution had failed almost as soon as it had begun? That most of the altruistic optimists who had formed the original Assembly had rapidly found themselves sidelined by those whose motives were corrupted by the sweet, addictive flavor of power.

He was in no doubt that there were men and women who were equally as starry eyed about the coming of the Snow Queen's regime. Believing that the equalizing excesses of the Republic would now be swept away and that a new era would emerge where there was a place for everyone within the freshly imposed hierarchy of the social spectrum. An era where everyone once more accepted his or her place without question.

Didn't they realize that what was coming was far worse that anything they'd seen before? That the social injustices which brought about the revolution in the first place were naught compared to the cold tyranny that was about to befall them under the Queen's icy grip?

Pulling on his heavy winter overcoat the Inquisitor gave an incredulous shake of his head and grinned smugly. What did he care? He would prosper in any political climate. Over the years he had assumed dozens of fictitious aliases. He relished the intrigue and deception involved in constructing a fresh identity to protect the anonymity of his true name.

Straightening his collar he took a last nostalgic look at the interior of the office that had given him so much sadistic pleasure over the past twelve months. Closing his eyes for a moment he remembered the power had held over those he had tortured. The power over life and death. He fancied that he could still hear the sweet echo of their agonized screams. After a moment he opened the door and walked along the corridor to the stairwell that would lead him down to the execution yard.

Outside it was bitterly cold. Needles of sleet, blown on the howling wind, stung at his face. The snow, which was thigh high on the guards and their prisoners, came up to his chest. Shivering and pulling the collar of his coat tight around his neck he ploughed his way across the yard, passing the multitude of snow covered humps where all the unnamed and nameless lay beneath unmarked burial mounds.

Near the blood stained wall the four remaining prisoners were being lashed to wooden posts ready for the members of the firing squad to perform their swansong. He observed them now with a wicked gleam in his eye. A pair of ill tempered and grotesquely disfigured sisters.

They had spent all of their incarceration haranguing and baiting each other through the bars of their cells and even now were rallying insults back and forth.

Next to them stood a decrepit old man, addled with senility. He was butt naked, his quivering flesh turning decidedly blue as he insistently declared that he was in fact dressed in all of his imperial finery. And finally a woman that he could not for the life him place. A princess of some sort — weren't they all — perhaps the one with the alleged pea under the mattress or possibly the one who had supposedly kissed a frog.

It didn't matter a jot to the Inquisitor. None of them would be given the satisfaction of hearing their names pronounced out loud before the triggers were pulled. When he read out their death sentences he would simply refer to each as citizen and let them die with the knowledge of how unimportant and irrelevant they had become.

"Sir." the Sergeant at Arms called over the bawl of the wind. "The prisoners are present and ready."

To his left the men of the execution squad were meticulously checking their rifles. The Inquisitor's little legs churned as he ploughed a furrow into the deep snow. Once this last task was done he would simply turn and disappear into the blizzard. And the Inquisitor would be no more. History rewritten once more.

First though, let these four specimens tremble at the name one last time. He approached the roughly bound prisoners and as he did so the woman whose identity he could not quite remember looked up and stared him straight in the eye.

"I know that little man!" she spat. "I know exactly who he is!"

"Of course you do," said the Sergeant at Arms. "He is the People's Inquisitor."

"He's a deceiver!" she spat. "A cheat and a swindler! A stealer of children!"

The Inquisitor ran his hand anxiously over his greasy hair and shook away the snow that had built up around his shoulders. Who was she? He felt positive that he aught to know her. Just as she claimed to know him. But suddenly a dense fug seemed to cloud his thoughts. He couldn't think straight.

"Gag her!" he said, stifling the panic that threatened to break in his voice. "Shut her up! She's knows what's about to happen and it has driven her crazy!"

The Sergeant at Arms barked an order to one of his men, who in turn, grabbed the woman by the hair and tried to stuff a dirty rag into her mouth. Despite the ropes tied around her wrists and ankles she fought like a wildcat, screaming and spitting at him. When finally it seemed as if he was about to win the battle she bit him so hard that he staggered away clutching a bloodied digit that dripped crimson droplets to stain the white snow.

"I know you!" she yelled. "I know your true name! Deceiver! Child stealer!"

Suddenly the Inquisitor realized who she was.

And how she knew him.

She had to be silenced before it was too late.

"Give me your pistol!" he barked at the Sergeant at Arms. "I'll finish this one myself!"

"I know your name," insisted the prisoner. "I know it and I'm going to speak it out loud."

The Sergeant at Arms fumbled with his holster.

"Hurry up, man!" shrieked the Inquisitor, his face turning purple with rage.

"Stiltskin!" cried the prisoner. "Rumpelstiltskin! Rumpelstiltskin is your name!"

At that the heads of the other three prisoners snapped upright from their slumped positions. Suddenly no longer befuddled the naked emperor spoke a different version of the Inquisitor's true name, in a far older tongue.

"Rumpenstunchen!"

At the sound of this the ugly sisters began to keen and wail, flailing their heads blindly this way and that. "Rumpelstiltskin! Rumpelstiltskin!" they screamed as loudly as all the poor children ever screamed when their parents told them of the wicked little man who would come for them if they carried on misbehaving.

The guards stopped what they were doing.

The Sergeant at Arms froze with his pistol half way drawn from his holster.

All eyes fell upon the Inquisitor.

"She's mad," he said, laughing out loud to show just how ridiculous the very suggestion was. He turned to the Sergeant at Arms. Almost pleading now. "She's mad, you see. She doesn't know what she's saying. She's lost her grip on reality."

The Sergeant just looked at him - jaw hanging slack. When the Inquisitor took a step towards him he shuffled backwards in the snow, as if the Inquisitor had somehow become suddenly contagious.

I know exactly what he's thinking, thought the Inquisitor. Rumpelstiltskin? A name on the list compiled by the Assembly. A name with a proscribed tale linked to it. A dangerous subversive. An undesirable miscreant. A fugitive from the swift and righteous justice of the glorious revolution. One of the Republic's most wanted dissidents. Here? In the headquarters of the People's Commissariat? Infiltrating the higher echelons of the officer corps?

Suddenly a dark shadow fell upon the snow-covered courtyard, oozing across it like a taint of oil. He looked up to the sky. Four and twenty monstrous black birds were circling high above the city, descending ever lower with each circuit, cawing menacingly as the beat of their huge dark wing cut swathes through the blizzard.

The Snow Queen was on her way.

The gates of the Citadel would not hold out much longer.

"Rumpelstiltskin is his name!" repeated the prisoner with studied venom.

"Kill her!" he screeched back. "Shoot her now. Shoot them all!"

No one moved.

The blackbirds came circling down ever lower, cawing with vicious beaks spread wide.

"Rumpenstunchen, Rumpenstunchen, Rumpenstunchen," raved old naked emperor.

The Inquisitor could feel the name gnawing powerfully into the very essence of him. The age-old wrath began boiling in his belly like blistering oil. Impossible to contain a long suppressed tantrum exploded out of him with such force that his little legs jumped at least two feet into the air, catapulting him out of the snow. A billow of snow puffed around him as he landed heavily on his back.

He gnashed his teeth and tried to stand upright again. He tore at his hair. He flailed his arms around and punched at invisible assailants. He kicked up fat clumps of snow this way and that across the courtyard. As his anger intensified he could feel hives and blisters and pus filled boils breaking out all over his furious face.

"Rumpenstunchen!"

"Rumpelstiltskin!"

"Kill them! Kill them! Kill the lot of them!" he raged and ranted.

His head went into a crazy, comic convulsion.

It felt as if it would shake right off his shoulders.

He shook so wildly that it was a wonder he didn't split himself in two.

Through blurred vision he saw the Sergeant at Arms aiming his pistol.

The Sergeant's hand was all a tremble.

He looked like a man about to put a mad dog out of its misery.

"Rumpelstiltskin," he whispered and pulled the trigger.

David Turnbull *is the author of a children's fantasy novel featuring dragon hunters and airships –* The Tale of Euan Redcap. *His short fiction has appeared in numerous magazines and anthologies, both online and in print. His most recent magazine publication was in* Lissette's Tales of the Imagination. *Recent anthologies include* Dandelions of Mars, *the Whortleberry Press tribute to Ray Bradbury and the forthcoming* Black Apples *anthology due for release shortly by Belladonna Press - as well as the forthcoming* Astrologica *anthology on Alchemy Press. He is member of Clockhouse London Writers.*

CLAWS

Marie Michaels

1

There is a city where metal grows like trees to rake the sky with silver fingers. At the center of this steel forest, people move in surges and currents that swirl under sun and moon. There are places where lights glitter without cease in every fathomable color, and others in perpetual dark. Countless stories are borne by the friction of countless passings of people in the midst of looming metal.

But where the silver trees crumble and the hard roads crack, night winds blow the streets empty except for the bravest, the most foolish and most desperate. Malice lurks in alleys, awaiting the vulnerable passer-by. Most denizens of this place have a story of this cruelty, perhaps as the victim and perhaps as the predator.

Some have both.

11

There are many neighborhoods in this city that are ignored by those fortunate enough to live elsewhere and forgotten by those who have escaped. In one of these neighbourhood there is a girl like so many, who was not born there but has always lived in a place like it. When sunlight flooded the cracked roads and neighbors strolled and gossiped, Beatrice liked the street in spite of its broken teeth and bruises, but she hated it at night. Two years ago, a man had followed her to the darkest place in the dark street, between a walled-off lot and an abandoned home, and demanded everything valuable she had. When she produced little of value, he left her bruised and terrified on the fractured sidewalk. Since that winter night, she feared to be alone here and feared even more to see others during her short walk home.

There was nothing unusual to mark that night before violence shattered the stillness, just as there was nothing to warn Beatrice of what would happen this night. But her heart beat hard and fast as the silent snowflakes fell. After a glance over her shoulder, she passed the place where the man had come upon her. As she did every night, she remembered the black mouth of the gun, the anger in his eyes, and the ringing shock of the blow that sent her to the frozen ground when he saw his meager spoils.

The street was empty. She passed the place in peace and saw the door to her safe haven. Her heart lifted, and she consigned the man to memory again. She fingered the keys she held ready.

A scream tore through the night. She froze and stared into the garden behind a chain link fence where the noise had come. Voices erupted in her head. Her mother's told her to run home and call the police, though Beatrice had little confidence in them. A second voice gibbered in fear, remembering gravel under her cheek and the sharp weight of the man's boot through her thin coat. Another shriek burst from the dark depths of the garden, this one laced with tears. A third voice seized hold of her and sent her charging through the gate, hot with rage. The sobbing ahead masked her footsteps.

A bulky figure hunched over a mass on the ground. Beatrice heard the man mutter and watched him reach out a slap the mass — a quaking girl — so hard that the crack of flesh on flesh echoed through the garden. Beatrice heard herself in the girl's cries. She had dreamed a hundred bloody dreams of revenge, and if this wasn't the same man, he was worse.

She ran forward and tackled the man, diving and wrapping her arms around his knees as she fell. Something fell away from him and winked silver in the starlight before disappearing in the shadows around the girl. Fury gave her strength to wrestle the man flat on his back, pin his arms with her elbows, and ram her knee as hard as she could between his legs. This time he screeched, higher and louder than the girl had, like a pig being butchered alive. Beatrice curled her fist, ready to smash it into the man's face.

"Get up," the girl whispered behind her. She was not angry or afraid. When Beatrice stood, she saw a skinny woman clad in tight jeans and a shredded pink satin jacket. Smiling. "Stand back." A revolver dangled from her hand before she slipped it into the pocket of her jacket.

The man snarled at them as he regained his breath. To Beatrice's horror, the girl knelt beside him. "Shut up," she crooned. "I warned you, didn't I?" Beatrice waited for the man to overpower the girl and punish them both... but when he struggled, the girl pushed and held him down like a cat trapping a mouse by its tail. "I warned you," she repeated.

A series of loud popping noises, and the man gasped. Beatrice leaned forward and could have sworn that she saw the girl's hands, transformed into eagle's talons, wrinkled yellow claws with wickedly curved black nails. She punctured his coat. If not for the cold and hot, sick taste of bile in the back of throat, Beatrice was sure she would have fainted. The girl turned her head to give Beatrice a long, slow smile.

The man flailed his arms, but the girl's arm moved with a swiftness Beatrice could not follow. She sliced the air between the man's arms and raked her black nails across the man's face. His voice was a wet gurgle when he shouted. A minute later, he lay still. The girl stood and took two steps toward Beatrice. Dark in the moonlight, blood spurted along the lines of the man's face.

"You were not afraid of him," the girl said. Her pale eyes locked onto Beatrice.

"I heard you screaming," Beatrice said. "I couldn't just do nothing. But listen, we gotta get outta here. Whoever finds this dude's gonna have a lotta questions we don't need." Steam rose from the man's head. Beatrice tried not to look at the girl's hands.

A flame lit behind the girl's eyes, which Beatrice saw were grey like an overcast winter day, as she lunged to grab Beatrice's wrist. "So angry," the girl murmured. "Such dark dreams in your heads." The girl's hands were knobby and hard. Bright fire shot through the mists of her eyes.

Beatrice tried to pull away, but the girl's grip tightened until the bones of her wrist ground together. "Goddammit lady, that hurts!" she cried out. Her voice shuddered.

Lightning danced in the girl's eyes. Her breath was sharp with cinnamon. "You loved hurting that nasty man, didn't you? You would do it again if you could. Avenge your hurts over and over. Never run scared down an empty street."

She hissed in Beatrice's ear. "I can help you do it." The tips of her claws grazed Beatrice's arm, and she looked down to see the powerful, ugly talons indenting her flesh.

"Oh shit." Her vision disintegrated, and she sagged against the fence. Sweat beaded along her hairline.

The man stirred and moaned. Beatrice found herself filled with that rushing anger again. For a moment she could taste the blood that had filled her mouth those two years ago. She still had a scar inside her cheek.

"Yes," she said. Cold air burned her lungs. "Help me." Her tongue traced the jagged line of the scar. "Help me stop being afraid."

The girl told Beatrice to cut her hands. She bit her neat white teeth into the yellow flesh of her claws and tore them from her milk pale wrists. A thin trickle of something dark soaked the girl's satin sleeves as she spat the claws into Beatrice's trembling hands.

"Wear them once, and they're yours until we meet again. They'll hide as you require them to, but only I can remove them." The girl bared her teeth at Beatrice, perhaps in a smile. "Enjoy. And run."

Beatrice ran. Her hands shook as she unlocked her door and slipped inside. Her keys and the claws clattered to her coffee table and came away crimson.

111

There was, at last, a free day and sunshine. Beatrice was happy to stare into windows as she strolled home with a bag of books. She passed bars too fashionable for her timidity and restaurants of the sort her mother abhorred, from which emanated a greasy aroma at once seductive and nauseating.

There was a muttered voice from her right. "Heeeeey whassup." Without moving her head, Beatrice glimpsed the man who had spoken. He was lean and hidden beneath a navy hooded sweatshirt and a crisp baseball cap. He slouched against faded red brick. The traffic light changed, and a honking stream trapped her on the curb.

Her mother handled this sort of thing with the grace of a queen. Girls her age laughed, made loud noises of disgust, or sometimes flirted back. But no one had ever spoken of it to Beatrice, so all too often these encounters left her embarrassed, angry, and somehow ashamed.

The man continued. "Yeah, I'm talking to you. Whassup, mama."

Beatrice's hands clenched inside her pockets. Something sharp poked her, and she remembered. *Avenge your hurts, again and again.*

He pushed off the wall, and Beatrice felt his shadow fall upon her. His voice sharpened. "What's wrong wichoo?"

Inside her pocket, she grabbed the claws and wished for some of the courage that had pushed her forward that night.

"Fuckin' stuck-up oreo bitch."

With that too-familiar insult, a rush of anger Beatrice clamped down on the claws. They crackled like fall leaves, and a spasm erupted in her hands. They strained and popped like she was having a fit, and suddenly they were *strong* and she knew what to do.

"The fuck..." Sensing that something had changed, the man stumbled away from her.

Traffic slowed. The light changed. A path opened up, but Beatrice turned toward the man. He recoiled as she threw herself forward and pressed him against the wall. Power and possibilities crackled in the ugly bones of the claws. She pressed the talons against his throat hard enough to dent the skin.

"That is not the way you speak to ladies." Her voice was careful and quiet. His eyes widened, and his mouth worked silently. She slipped into more casual speech, with a grin tugging at her lips. "You feel me? Have some respect."

"Hey man, get away from me, you crazy-ass-"

With a small movement, she cut off the next slur on its way out. "I said," she spat between gritted teeth, "you feel me? Respect. It ain't hard." His blood pounded under her hand as his breath shook.

"Yeah," he squeaked. She eased her grip slightly. "You, I feel you." Though she guessed he was at least ten years older than her, his terror made him suddenly much younger. She stepped back and watched him rub his throat and scamper away.

Delight filled her, and she wanted to skip across the street. She looked down at her hands, now adjusting the strap of her bag. She laughed aloud to see that they were back to normal — brown and bumpy with fine bones and raised veins.

This was going to be fun.

1⌄

There was a Sunday, and Sundays were two things for Beatrice: Mass and her weekly visit with her mother, Jacqueline. Jacqueline did not know what to make of Beatrice these days. Beatrice was tired every Sunday at Mass, and on this day she trudged to her mother's apartment with ill grace.

There was anger in Jacqueline's loud, rattling preparation of the tea. "You were asleep during Mass." Her voice was sharp. "For the past month, you have been asleep at Mass. You stay out late on Saturday nights? With boys?"

Beatrice smiled down at her nails. The claws stirred.

"Yes and no," she said at last. Her easy tone and evasion infuriated Jacqueline. Where was the girl who used to blush at the mention of boys and curl into herself at any hint of maternal disapproval? "Not the way you think."

"It is not right." Her mother stirred her tea so hard it slopped into the saucer painted with roses. "Are you one of these *women*," her tone suggesting a stronger word she was too gracious to utter, "who stays out with boys all night? It is not safe. You should know that after what that man did to you."

Anger simmered inside Beatrice. Did her mother think she forgot that night for a single day? Forgot how she'd stayed weeping on the ground for half an hour after the man left? She had been unable to move for terror he would return. Jacqueline blamed her for being stupid enough to be in that man's way that night.

Her fingernails grew dark and sharp and left identical grooves in the side of the table. "I ain't forgotten anything." She took a deep breath and forced the smile her mother hated back to her face. "But things are changing where I live. I ain't scared no more." Her mother sniffed. "In fact, I think it's other people who should be scared."

Jacqueline grabbed Beatrice's wrist. "What are you talking about? I hope you have not done something very foolish just to make me angry." Her eyes scoured Beatrice, and for a moment, Beatrice's courage flickered. She used to think her mother could read her mind.

Beatrice tugged her hand back. "Mama, I don't even know what you're talking about." She barked a short laugh as she realized what her mother was too decorous to say aloud. "I ain't dating no damn gangbanger."

Jacqueline sighed again and leaned back in her chair. "You know that I worry. You are strange lately, Bea. Headstrong. Not so obedient to your mother."

Bitterness puckered Beatrice's mouth. Only her mother would praise her for a quality after she had lost it. "You're right," she said. "I am different. You wouldn't understand, but trust me, I'm okay."

Her mother regarded her over the gold lip of the tea cup. "You are not my little girl anymore."

$\vee$

There were night and solitude, at last. When darkness came, Beatrice's weariness evaporated. She knew she should sleep to face the coming week, but her visit with her mother had stirred her up. What she could not tell her mother was that she was making the streets safe, night by night. She carried her prized brown-and-tan Louis Vuitton bag and browsed on her phone down feared side streets. Sundays were her favorite day for hunting because the streets emptied early.

Yet she could never predict how much time would pass as she hunted. Sometimes hours passed in her slow stroll, and sometimes she only had to cross the avenue before acquiring a shadow. She sought streets with empty windows and barren lots.

This time, she wandered for half a mile before the familiar tingle prickled her skin. The claws had enhanced her hearing or perhaps given her a sixth sense that warned her long before anyone could approach her. A bicycle squeaked behind her, slowing and then stopping as the man – it was always a man – stalked her. She bared her teeth at the night.

The man's gait was efficient, quiet, and slightly uneven as if he carried a weight on one side. Beatrice's heart raced, and warmth melted through her limbs. She spotted a half-constructed steel and glass tower and stopped there on the pretence of a furious bout of texting. The claws thrumming underneath her skin made it a delicate operation.

"Hey," he grunted, coming up beside her. "You got the time." The question was a flat, unconvincing act.

"Sure!" she bubbled. She relished these last seconds of her role. "It's nine—" As she spoke, she turned to face him and took in the knitted hat pulled low, the scarf wrapped around his mouth, and the sweatshirt that did not quite cover a bulge at his waistband.

"Gimme your stuff," he said before she could finish. "All of it."

When he took a step toward her, Beatrice did not hide her glee. The speed of her arm delighted her as the claws burst out of her skin and slashed bloody rents across the man's face. She shredded his scarf and opened his cheek deeply enough that he would dribble food when he ate. For now she would avoid his eyes unless he became... difficult.

He screamed and drooled blood as he tottered away from her. With one hand he fished blindly for the gun in his pants.

"Don't wanna do that unless you don't want no more kids," she said in a voice loud enough to carry over his moans. "You think I won't do it?"

He bubbled curses at her and yanked the handle of his weapon out of his waistband. Beatrice leapt forward and landed in a deep lunge. She swatted the gun away, ripping open his jeans. The cuts in his fingers were shallow, but the proximity of her claws to his pelvis set him shrieking. He stumbled away, gibbering about devil-women.

She retrieved from her purse the baby wipes she carried for this reason, wrapped one around the handle of the gun, and threw it over a limp wooden fence. Blood and success intoxicated her. She chased the man back to his bicycle and tugged him backward by the tattered sleeve of his sweatshirt. "Next time you cross some helpless little thing, I will kill you," she hissed. "You believe me." He cringed against the concrete, babbling. After that, she knew she would believe anything she said.

Beatrice strolled home, only mildly disappointed not to meet anyone else during the walk. She smiled as she collapsed into sleep.

V1

There was spring, and the community garden bloomed with buttery daffodils. Beatrice had to travel further to find new victims. Not victims, she told herself, targets. Predators who needed to know what it was to be prey.

There was a duo, for the first time. One of them eyed her as she crossed a half-lit intersection, where his partner tried to hide behind a dumpster. When they followed her inside a bank lobby to an ATM, she didn't bother waiting for them to attack. She flew like a hummingbird around a lumbering pair of elephants, jabbing and retreating. They egged each other on. What little mercy she may have had leeched out of her with every renewed assault. Their mingled blood washed the floor red.

These days, Beatrice needed a new neighborhood. She walked for hours through a tranquil night. Tired and thirsty, she stepped inside the neon entrance of an all-night bodega to buy a bottle of something cold and sweet. A man stood behind her at the counter. He took half a step closer to her. Beatrice flexed her fingers in anticipation, paid, and slipped into the night. Quiet footsteps followed her around the corner.

"'sup mami," the man said. His voice was velvety and low just over her shoulder.

She whirled and pinned him against the wall by his throat. The claws of her other hand rested against his side, leanly muscled under his jacket. He chuckled, but his laughter died as she pressed the razor tips of the talons hard enough to snag his shirt. His blood thundered hot under her fingers.

"Fuck's wrong with you!" he sputtered. "I was trynna be nice!"

Beatrice's lip curled. She'd heard it all before, all the excuses. It was compliment. Most girls liked it. She was being too sensitive. How else were men supposed to talk to women? She was viciously sick of it.

"You scared," she whispered. "Yeah? I used to be scared all the time. You ever think how that feels?" Her claws pressed harder, scratching his skin. He keened. "You want some dude sneaking up on you and talking like he wants to do some shit you ain't interested in? How do I know you'll hear me if I say no? Y'all ain't thinking with your heads." She let her free hand glide down his shirt. "Maybe I should just clear your mind."

The man froze with terror when she let her claws sink into the denim at his thighs. He stank with fear, quivered like a trapped moth. He would tell his friends, and they would tell theirs. Word would spread, and the streets would finally be safe, thanks to just a little swipe she could take right now. If he survived.

Tears leaked from the corners of his eyes. "I won't do it again, lady, I swear! Fuck, don't do it, I'm sorry!" His voice broke. The rushing blood under her hands filled her brain. He started praying in a language she did not understand, and for a moment she was transported back to her mother's tidy home and the rosaries she said nightly.

The image jarred her. She surveyed the scene as if from the security camera that gazed with a cracked eye. The man was blubbering and whispering apologies. She saw traces of baby fat in his cheeks and realized he was younger than she. He crumpled to the ground when she backed away. The store owner stared at her as she passed the open door of the bodega.

The ghost of his heartbeat beat beneath her claws. Her stomach lurched at the memory of his brown eyes. The unsated talons flexed at the sight of every man she saw on her long walk home. For so long she had gone out hunting every night, and now to return without blood on her claws...

She stumbled to the community garden and collapsed atop a mound of green shoots. *Such dark dreams*, the woman had said she she'd touched Beatrice.

The claws stirred again as loathing choked her. The black talons glittered in the starlight, striking against the shrivelled yellow flesh when she clutched her wrists. She clenched her jaw and closed her eyes. Inky liquid that bubbled forth when she squeezed her claws. Pain flared like lightning and roared like thunder even as she thrilled at the wetness of blood.

Footsteps crushed the shoots beside her. "I told you," a familiar voice said with the warmth of an indulgent mother. "Only I can remove them. You tired of my gift already?"

Beatrice forced her eyes open to see the same tattered pink satin jacket and storm grey eyes above her. "I gotta stop." Her voice was ragged. "I don't care. I'll do it myself."

The woman laughed. "You don't care so much you're snivelling in the dirt. I'm disappointed, Beatrice. Do you know what you could have accomplished in a year? Imagine this city, finally clean of those vermin that prey on the weak. You would have been a hero."

"I would have been a murderer." Beatrice pictured the boy's face. She heard again his whispered prayers. "It wasn't worth it."

The woman knelt. Fire flashed in her pale eyes. "Tell that to the next girl." Her teeth flashed in a grimace. "Revenge used to be so much easier. I'll take my gift back, but it won't be free this time. Everything they gave you, they take back. It won't be pretty."

Beatrice let herself imagine the future the woman had seen, then bowed her head. She could already feel her old weakness creeping back. "Take them."

She could not scream for fear of raising alarm as pain ripped through her like nothing she had ever known. She prayed for unconsciousness, but agony washed over her again and again like an incoming tide. Fire seared her arms. At last she felt something other than pain in her hands – dirty and sticky grass underneath her fingernails.

She was alone.

Her body was clumsy and slow when she stood. The night was darker and the shadows bigger. The tingle of the claws had vanished, leaving only heaviness. Exhaustion dragged at her. She could feel deep bruises gather beneath her skin.

When she limped to her door and fished in her purse for her keys, every touch against her hands burned. Her fingers were so weak that she dropped the keys twice before fitting them into the lock. Tears pooled in her eyes at the pain. She moaned when she brushed on a light switch and stifled a shriek when lamplight flooded the room. Her hands were twisted and knobby, thick and scarred like they'd been broken over and over. Underneath it, a yellowish tinge lurked beneath her brown skin and the edges of nails flashed black.

She cradled her hands to her chest. As tears slid down her cheeks, she discovered that she could smile. Weak as they were, now ugly and burning with transformation, her hands were hers again. And maybe she was stronger than she thought.

꒰ ꒱

Marie Michaels *is a lawyer by day and a nerd pretty much all the time. Originally from the Midwest, she now lives among the glittering lights and slinking shadows of New York City. She writes short stories and novels about the strange, surprising, terrifying, and occasionally wonderful happenings that take place beneath the skin of the City and beyond the bounds of our world.* "Claws" *is her first fictional publication. She tweets about sci-fi, fantasy, and feminism at @lavidanerdy. She is currently brainstorming her eleventh NaNoWriMo novel.*

EIDERDOWN

Mark A. France

Maizy Lankton plucked the small crimson bead from her cheek with the gentle touch of a fingertip. Holding her hand in front of her face, she watched the droplet of blood descend the length of her finger; a stark color to her ashen skin. Her eyes widened at the realization that she had not sustained any injury and the blood on her hand was not hers.

Dragging her hand down the front of her blouse, she turned her eyes to the small boy who lay in a heap upon the oak wood floor. His little hands were partially clenched into fists and his eyes starred off into shadows as his head lay at an awkward angle. A rosy gash crossed from the side of his temple to just above his right ear, blood seeping into his auburn locks and the floorboards beneath him. A hand-stitched teddy bear lay by his side.

Maizy's lips trembled as she took a tentative step forward then dropped to her knees. Her tongue betrayed her as she tried to speak his name, but could not link syllables together, midst the sobs which shuddered through her.

Hand-over-hand, she moved towards her son, paying no heed to the splinters that pierced her flesh. Kneeling before the boy, she lifted her trembling hands to her mouth in an attempt to stifle a cry, but a mournful wail lifted up through her throat and escaped into the silence of the single-room house.

The light around her began to dim. Darkness closed in on the edge of Maizy's vision as she continued to wail, her eyes not daring to fall away from her son. Gulping air, she slowly sunk down further where she knelt, her nails finding purchase on the surface beneath her and digging into the floorboards. Every scream pushed her closer to fainting, until her voice hitched with a knot in her chest and the trembling wails turned to choking sobs. She gagged, then spat up a stream vomit laced with blood; her throat raw and bleeding.

As if time had slowed to a crawl, she watched her hand reach out towards the boy, hovering over his still chest. She urged herself to touch him, to find out whether life had truly fled his small body. Tears streamed down her face, cutting rivulets through patches of soot on her cheeks. Inching closer, her fingers splayed, her hand drifting inches from the child's black and white striped pullover.

Then there was a knock at the door. The minute vibration sent a chill down Maizy's arms, her outstretched hand flinching back as if she had just touched a hot flame. Her eyes darted to the door, mind reeling. Sweat broke out on her brow as her heart pounded in her chest. She didn't realize she was holding her breath until her head began to swim in the afternoon sun and a hazy grey edged her vision. She exhaled quickly, and then filled her lungs with the stagnant air within the four walls of the house.

Standing slowly, she took a tentative step towards the door, her legs trembling as tiny pinpricks nipped at her toes, moving to the heels of her feet. She thought about crossing to the window facing the front of the house, but knew that any disturbance of the worn drapes would draw attention. Instead, she sidled up to the door and placed her hands on either side of the frame, positioning herself in front of a small knothole that allowed her to peer out on the front lot of the house.

A shadow lay in overgrown grass and weeds, its owner just out of sight.

Maizy took hold of the door's knob, the coolness of the brass kissing lightly against her splintered hand. Turning it slowly, she heard the bolt disengage. Peering back over her shoulder, a single tear broke free as she watched dust motes drift down about her son - her only child - and wished that today could be yesterday once again.

The door creaked open and sunlight chased away the shadows that crowded about Maizy's feet. Stepping out, she pulled the door closed behind her. She was greeted by a small woman garbed in a long, cotton dress.

Evelyn Mulberry had recently turned sixty-five, yet the years had been unkind to her. Just under five feet tall, her height was betrayed by an arthritic malady which caused her to hunch forward as she supported herself with a cane made of sandalwood; a gift from her great aunt. Her skin, which shown with liver spots, was dark with sun and gave off the appearance of worn leather. Her pointy nose struck forward like a beak, while her lips were slivered moons of pale violet. Eyes, once a brilliant hazel with gold flecks, were now sunken orbs diseased with cataracts.

The old woman peered up at Maizy, her brow creased with worry.

"Are you alright, Ms. Lankton?" Evelyn said as she drew a step closer, the tip of her cane clacking off one of the sunken flagstones.

"Missus," Maizy corrected. "And thank you, yes, I am fine."

Evelyn tilted her head to the side, her clouded eyes searching for truth in Maizy's expression. Nodding slowly, she peered about the small acreage of the yard, before returning her gaze back to Maizy.

"I came out here to talk Church business, but I heard you cry out." Evelyn shifted her weight from one foot to the other.

Maizy dipped her shoulders. "I've been having a rough time as of late, and today has been no different." She looked towards the ground, unconsciously swiping another stray tear from her cheek. "I haven't heard from Paul in weeks and the wait is unbearable."

She lifted her eyes to Evelyn as her thoughts drifted to the events that led up to this moment. Maizy's chest hitched as she took a deep breath. Those milky eyes paused briefly, before Evelyn turned her head towards the start of the footpath. She lifted her chin in the direction of a rotund woman who huddled under a sheltering pine.

"Luck would have it that I'd be accompanied by Mrs. Wexford," she sneered, returning her gaze to Maizy. "They all think I'm blind, but I can see better than the lot of them." Evelyn's voice had dropped to a whisper.

Maizy lifted her hand to wave, but let it fall to her side when Mrs. Wexford turned away. She knew she was not a favorite at the Beloved Grace Methodist Church, but her husband had formed a strong bond with the pastor shortly after their first visit several years back. It didn't make sense to rock the boat when Paul was happy. And it didn't make sense to upset Evelyn, especially since she was married to the pastor of their Faith.

Evelyn's eyes drifted down with Maizy's, until she exclaimed, "My dear, you've hurt yourself."

Reaching out, the old woman took hold of Maizy's hand and turned her palm skywards. Blood speckled the flesh, several large blotches drying in the summer air. Knotted fingers exposed the damage caused by the wrecked floor of the house. Maizy stood motionless for a brief moment as ghost-riddled eyes drifted over the crimson-stained wounds that mapped the skin below her wrist. Quickly, she snatched her hand away and tucked it behind her back.

"It's nothing. I just moved some firewood at the back of the house and was about to wash up." Maizy brought her hand around in front of her and folded it into the other.

"You best be more careful. Perhaps you should let Mrs. Wexford have a look at them." Evelyn nodded in agreement with her own suggestion.

"There's no need. I can manage on my own."

The older woman sighed heavily. "And Benjamin, how is he?"

Maizy glanced at the door, her eyes remaining there for the briefest of moments. Turning back to Evelyn, she forced a smile. "He's been feeling a bit ill as of late."

"That's a shame. I was having some women from the church over this afternoon and was hoping he would be able to accompany me to the parsonage to sing for us. He has such a beautiful voice."

"Unfortunately, he needs his rest." Maizy took a tentative step away from Evelyn.

"He will be able to perform this Sunday, will he not?"

Icy fingers traced down Maizy's spine. Her head ached horribly and her eyes seemed to lose focus. The sun was too bright, the air cloyingly thick. Evelyn quickly reached out, steadying Maizy as she began to lose her balance.

"My dear, are you alright?" Evelyn's voice seemed far away.

Rubbing her temple, Maizy shook her head, as if the action would clear her thoughts. "I'm fine. Too much sun, I think. Or maybe a touch of what Benjamin has. Maybe I should lie down."

"Would you like me to fetch Dr. Peterson?"

"No. No, I'll be alright."

Evelyn gave a single nod. "It'd be no trouble at all." Her voice, while showing concern, was laced with an icy undertone.

"I'm *fine*," Maizy snapped, the words drawing attention from Mrs. Wexford who moved from beneath the shade of the pine.

Stunned by her own outburst, Maizy cupped her injured hands over her mouth, tears welling up and on the verge of spilling over. Evelyn glared at her, the twin white pools in her eyes seeming to engulf her with pity and disgust.

Turning away, Evelyn limped down the footpath, her cane leading the way through the unkempt grass and the choking weeds. Her chin lifted skywards as she watched a large crow take to the air from the branch of a sunburned oak. Stopping abruptly, she spun back towards Maizy, her agility defying her bodily afflictions.

"You *will* have your son's wardrobe prepared for church on Sunday. And you *will* make sure that he is well and ready to sing for the congregation." Evelyn spoke sharply and with a commanding force, as if her words held more weight than others. "If it wasn't so important to the Ladies Fellowship, they would not have purchased the materials so that he might have suitable garments to wear for this special occasion. See that it is done."

Mrs. Wexford met her halfway up the footpath, tucking her arm under Evelyn's. Neither woman glanced back as Maizy watched them maneuver through the foliage that separated her property from the gravel road they had arrived on. Eventually, both figures disappeared behind a line of trees to the East.

Shaken and upset, Maizy turned away and towards her home. The house seemed so much smaller than she remembered. Misshapen vines crawled up the sides and spilled over the rooftop, cradling it in their embrace. Rotted pilings were all that remained of the front porch; the wood burned long ago on a chilly, winter's night.

She peered down at her bloodstained hands, before turning her gaze to the front door. Maizy tried to convince herself that it was all a bad dream, that the moment she entered the house, Benjamin would be sitting at the dining table playing with the checker board his father had given him just before being sent off to war.

Rusty hinges squealed as Maizy opened the door and the summer sun chased off encompassing shadows. Benjamin lay motionless where he had fallen, his face turned away to the opposite corner of the house. A wave of despair flooded through Maizy's body as she slowly walked over to where her son lay. Shoulders shuddering, she dropped down beside him and began to cry softly. Her hand, which had betrayed her before, lighted softly on her son's pullover.

"Oh, dear God, it was an accident," she cried softly to the silent room.

Cupping a hand behind his head, Maizy lifted the small boy into her lap, feeling the awkward weight of his limp body. A stray tear fell onto Benjamin's cheek, lingering there until Maizy kissed it away.

"I'm so, so sorry." Maizy gently rocked the boy, cradling him close to her chest. "My little Benjamin."

In life, Benjamin had been the light of Maizy's world; a rambunctious child who felt the need to get into mischief any chance he could. And while his play was often exuberant, he had a soft, kind side that often endeared him to those around him. Where his father had made friends at Beloved Grace through his commanding nature, Benjamin's lively spirit and angelic voice had made men and women fall in love with him.

Standing, Maizy carefully carried Benjamin to his small bed at the rear of the house. Laying him on the cotton mattress, she brushed his hair from his eyes. The life that had filled those deep blue pools had fled, chased away by her own hand. She wanted to turn back time; to go back to the moment when anger had overpowered her.

Earlier that morning, Benjamin had tried to put on a puppet show for her. He had gathered up his teddy bear and crafted little animals made from a torn sheet and bits of yarn. While Maizy busied herself with sewing and cleaning, Benjamin crouched behind the rusted-out icebox, having pinned a charcoal picture to the wall for his backdrop. He paraded his bear and miscellaneous creations back and forth in an attempt to amuse his mother, making up little songs and singing them as he played.

When he could not garner Maizy's attention, Benjamin moved to the edge of the table where his mother had piled various pieces of material and threads. Singing louder and being more animated with his toys, Benjamin tried desperately to share his imaginary world with his mother, but only succeeded in irritating her.

Maizy knew Benjamin missed his father and that he often felt lonely. There were no other children around to play with, except on Sundays at church. At times, he would have conversations with himself or talk to his imaginary friends. Recently, Maizy had found him sitting in the vegetable garden, his eyes puffy from crying. When she tried to console him, he had clung to her, sucking his thumb like he had when he was a baby.

It wasn't that she didn't want to have a relationship with her son; it was just hard to give him her full attention every minute of the day.

Soot dusted the floor like a gray carpet, bits of wood scattered about Maizy's feet as she prodded at the remnants of last night's cooking fire. Poker in hand, she prodded the inside of the iron stove, while holding open the metal grill. Shifting her weight, she lost her balance and the grill slammed down on the hand holding it open. Cursing, she yanked the poker out and gave the stove a quick lashing. As metal glanced off metal, Maizy cried out again.

From somewhere behind her, Benjamin laughed; a seven year olds amusement. With pain ebbing through her hand, she spun on her heels, the poker slashing the air around her until it met brief resistance. Benjamin had been standing behind her, his teddy bear clutched in his arms.

Maizy leaned forward and kissed Benjamin on the cheek. Finally, she brushed her hand over his eyelids, closing his dead stare into darkness. Laying his small hands on his chest, she placed her head on the pillow beside him and let her eyes drift shut.

Maizy stood in a vast field, butterflies lighting upon wild daisies and golden lilies. Somewhere in the distance, Benjamin sang a lilting lullaby, his sweet voice drifting upon a warm, summer breeze. As she waded amongst Queen Ann's Lace and swaying bellflowers, the foliage grew taller and her son's voice grew dimmer. Field thistles and biting sawgrass cut against her legs. When she could move forward no more, Maizy called out to her son, only to be met with soft crying, muffled by the dense growth. Maizy's heart ached as Benjamin's cries became more desperate. An owl called out somewhere nearby.

Maizy woke with a start, her dream lingering as she heard Benjamin's weeping fade into the darkness around her. Her back creaked as she sat up, a spike of pain shooting through her neck. The constant drone of chirping crickets filled the air, joined by the incessant croak of a bullfrog.

Cheeks wet with tears, Maizy traced her hands across the bed, feeling the small form of her son. Squeezing his hands, she stood and did her best to get her bearings. Hands outstretched, she shuffled across the floor, her body chilled by a cool breeze that spilled through the open front door.

When she found her way to the dining table, she traced her fingers along the surface, until they closed on a small oil lantern; next to it lie a wooden box of matches.

Once lit, the lantern cast an amber glow about the room, which died in the corners as shadows danced with the flickering flame. Peering out the front door, Maizy shivered as her eyes sought out the moon or a lone star, but could find none. She shut and latched the door, closing out the intruding night and whatever lay beyond the threshold of the door.

When she turned back to the room, her eyes went right to the bed and the small boy who lay in it. Her throat clenched shut, her heart pounding in her ears. Benjamin's head lay to the side, his eyes open, staring at her. As she moved towards her own bed, his eyes seemed to follow her. Stopping halfway, she switched her direction and quickly walked towards his still form. As she crossed the floor, the light from the lantern flickered, shadows twisting about Benjamin's prone body. As she neared him, she let out her breath.

His eyes were closed.

Maizy moved to the dining table, where she sat and attempted to rub warmth into her arms. Nervous energy made her rock forward and back, forward and back. She paused at every sound, listening.

When an hour had passed, she finally turned to the pile of material lying neatly on the table. With shaking hands, she pulled the cloth in front of her and retrieved a threaded needle from her pin cushion which was neatly tucked in one of Paul's old cigar boxes. As she began to piece Benjamin's outfit together, Maizy's attention was divided between a flitting moth that bobbed and weaved about the glowing lantern, and completing the project at hand.

When the clocks hour hand rested on the three and the minute hand divided the twelve, Maizy folded the finished outfit and carefully laid it on the tabletop. She pushed her chair away from the table and stood, looking down on the dark garments. In all her life, she never thought she would sew together the clothing her son would wear in death.

She lifted the outfit into her arms and walked to Benjamin's bed; he looked so small lying there, as if he were quietly sleeping.

A dark form danced across the wall, giant wings beating silently. Maizy shivered as the temperature dropped several degrees. Outside, the crickets ceased chirping and silence ruled the night. A flare of light drew Maizy's attention to the dining table as the lone moth fell upon the rough wood, its wings a dying flame.

Returning her gaze to her son, Maizy set down beside him, her eyes falling upon his cherub face. At one time, his cheeks had been flushed with life, but now, red and blue veins traced across translucent flesh. The jovial smile he had once shared was now faded, pale-blue, parted lips. The blood that had spilled from the wound to his temple had darkened to a flaking brown stain.

It didn't take long for Maizy to dress him in the garments she had sewn together. Rigor had been broken by the hands of the clock, but Maizy flinched back when she saw the maroon patches of pooled blood which shown on her son's underside. Once he was robbed in the cotton clothing, Maizy moved to her bed in the opposite corner of the room.

The trunk slid out from under the suspended mattress, its exterior covered in a layer of dust. Hinges cried out as Maizy lifted the lid and peered down at its contents. The dress she had worn on the day of her wedding moldered to the rear of the trunk. Several black and white photos lay beneath glass in wooden frames.

And then there was the hand-stitched eiderdown quilt; a gift from Paul's parents on their wedding day.

Maizy pulled the eiderdown quilt and wedding dress from the trunk. Spreading the quilt across the floor, she hefted her son into her arms and placed him on the feather duvet. Folding the edges over, Maizy kissed Benjamin's cheek before drawing the quilt over his face.

With her son bound in the eiderdown quilt, Maizy tore strips of material from her wedding dress, laying them in a pile next to her as she sat on the hardwood floor. Using the torn dress, Maizy knotted the shredded material around the top and bottom of the quilt, then tied two more lengths a quarter of the way to the middle.

The man-made cocoon flexed as Maizy carried it to the front door and laid it in the threshold. She snatched up the lantern, threw open the latch and lifted her son into her arms. As she stepped out into the night, a thin mist swirled about her legs like transparent fingers. Wading through overgrown grass and wildflowers, Maizy passed beneath several towering pines, before she came to the corroded lip of an old well.

Damp ground crumbled, bits of concrete and rock tumbling into the gaping hole in the ground. Rivulets of water cascaded down the interior walls, each droplet echoing up from the shallow reservoir below.

Maizy wrapped her arms around her son and held him close as rain began to fall. After what seemed like forever, she moved her son to the edge of the well and forced herself to look away as a portion of the eiderdown quilt disappeared into shadows. Before her hand let go, and her son's body plummeted into the dark abyss of the well, Maizy felt a slight movement within the duvet.

Silence filled the seconds before a shallow splash echoed up from the wells depths. Maizy teetered over the gaping maw, eyes wide. Her mind reeled as her hands scrabbled for a hold on the brick that encircled the manufactured chasm. Had wishful thinking made her imagine that her son was still alive, or had the chill in the air caused the muscles in her hand to spasm, driving false hope into her conscious mind? Or had Benjamin awoke from unconsciousness and the movement was a true sign of life?

"Benjamin!" Maizy screamed into the night, her face turned up to the sheets of rain that fell heavily against her skin. "Dear God, why have you done this to me?"

Maizy collapsed to the ground. Her fingers clawed through the viscous mud in front of her as exhaustion threaded itself to her very core.

∽✦∾

The sun peeked over the top of a line of trees to the east. Clouds parted and the humidity of the breaking day pressed down on Maizy as she struggled to stand, her body riddled with aches and pains. Wet earth slid down her unstable legs as she tried to hold her balance.

Picking up the lantern, Maizy turned away from the well and walked to the entrance of the house. She paused in the threshold and turned towards the overgrown path and the horizon beyond. On the other side of the gravel road lay a vast field of wheat. She squinted against the sun's rays as a shadowy form moved amongst the sun-washed grain. When she blinked, the figure was gone.

Maizy knew she needed sleep and that her heart was playing tricks through her mind. It was true that she wanted to see Benjamin bound across the field, or for Paul to come up behind her and wrap his arms about her waist, but she knew it was all wishful thinking; a punishment for taking her husband and son for granted. A painful mirage born of guilt

As she stepped into the house, Maizy closed the front door and let the coolness of the shadowed room wash over her. Securing the latch, she stripped the muddy clothing from her body, leaving it in a pile on the floor. Maizy bathed with the water that remained in the wash basin next to her bed, before she dressed and lay down on the thin, faded mattress. Her gaze drifted about the room, before it fell upon Benjamin's empty bed; he should have been lying there, sleeping.

Maizy lay there for a while, listening to the birth of a new day, while her heart died inside. Finally, she closed her eyes, and darkness, once again reigned over her.

಄

Maizy stirred from her sleep, her mind clouded with dying dreams. She pushed herself into a sitting position and let her feet dangle over the side of the bed. The room had taken on a chill, which eclipsed the warmth of the previous day. Sheets of rain danced across the roof; an ensemble of nature's percussion, joined by resonant rumbles of thunder. Little light shown through the front window as clouds masked the dying day.

Leaning forward, Maizy let her feet light upon the floor. A chill raced up her legs; a web of cold cast through her body. She snatched her feet back for a brief moment, biting down on the inside of her mouth, before placing them back on the unfinished hard wood. As she stood, the blanket that lay on the bed sighed to the floor.

Maizy leaned to pick up the blanket and noticed another swatch of material partially hidden under the lip of the bed. Tossing the blanket onto the mattress, she knelt and lifted the thin strip of cloth from where it lay. The texture was so familiar to her touch, its silkiness smooth between her fingers. The color was faded, but she recognized it as a piece from of her wedding dress. A portion of the material lay knotted and encrusted in mud.

Maizy cast the material away and turned towards the front door as a crack of thunder reverberated through the house. Something moved against the door, before a shadow obscured the window for the briefest of moments. Fear enveloped her as scenarios played out in her mind. Had Evelyn sent one of the men from the church to check on the welfare of her son? Or had somebody stumbled across the well and the body of Benjamin inside?

Throwing open the door, Maizy stepped out into the down pouring rain. A strong wind whipped against her, clutching at her clothing. Shadows ducked in and out from behind the surrounding trees as they swayed beneath the darkened sky. Maizy strained to see down the overgrown path, but could see no further than the first twenty feet. She clutched her hands about her shoulders and turned to head back into the house when she caught something out of the corner of her eye.

Bracing herself against the rain, Maizy stepped away from the entryway and walked towards a hemlock sapling growing alongside the house. Muddy earth oozed between her toes as she knelt beside the bundle tucked beneath the trees low-hanging branches. Her heart thudded in her ears as she pulled the eiderdown quilt out into the open, the duvet soaked with water.

Saturated, Maizy carried the quilt into the house and deposited it in a heap upon the floor. Turning away, she pulled at her hair, tears streaming down her cheeks. She questioned whether she had gone mad and this was all a delusion. All signs pointed to Benjamin being alive and having crawled from the watery grave she had given him, but it was impossible, she told herself. She had seen the blank stare in his lifeless eyes when she placed him within the eiderdown quilt. And she knew the fall alone would have taken the life of such a small child.

After lighting the lantern, Maizy grabbed a chair from beside the table and slammed it down next to the duvet; the sound was swallowed by a crack of thunder, a deafening roar that filled the room. Letting herself slump into the chair, Maizy folded her hands in her lap, binding her fingers tightly together. She remained where she was for nearly an hour, listening to the storm move off into the distance, while she tried to wrap her mind around the past day-and-a-half.

When the rain finally stopped falling, Maizy stood and lifted the quilt into her arms, a portion of the sodden duvet dragging across the floor as she moved to the cast iron stove. Throwing open the grate, she began to stuff the quilt into the stove's dark maw, crying out when half of it would not fit.

Overcome with emotion, Maizy reached for the poker, before she stopped midway, her hand dancing inches away from it. She shook her head from side to side, all the time her eyes remaining locked upon the metallic stoker. This is what you killed your son with, she told herself.

"My beloved Benjamin", she wept to the empty room. "My husband's son. My little boy with the angelic voice."

Her fingers closed about the handle of the poker as she snatched it from where it lay. Taking hold of it with both hands, she jabbed at the portion of the quilt that hung from the mouth of the stove. The metal hook at the end of the poker tore open seams and split the thin material, which spilled forth eiderdown feathers. When no more of the quilt could fit into the stove, Maizy dropped the poker to the floor with a clatter. Her breathing was heavy from the exertion. Sweat dampened her forehead.

She punished herself with thoughts of the past, of a time when there was no war and Paul strolled through the fields, his hand in hers; a time when Benjamin's happiness shown upon his face and his voice was as sweet as honey. Now, her mind was riddled with guilt; a self-hatred built upon the knowledge of what she had done and what she needed to do.

She had to flee. She couldn't remain here amongst the reminders of what she had done. Paul might return someday, but she would not be able to greet him upon his arrival; she would have to bear the burden of both losses for as long as she lived.

Maizy retrieved the box of matches from beside the lantern and returned to the stove. She lit the first match and held it to a shredded edge of the damp material. When the flame hushed out, she lit another, trying to find a bit of the duvet that had either partially dried or was not soaked through with rain. Her frustration escalated when several of the matches snapped apart as she struck them against the box.

"Damn you", she screamed as she threw the wooden box to the floor, its contents scattering as the container broke.

Feathers drifted about Maizy as she pulled the quilt from the stove and cast it into the middle of the room. She banged her knee on the edge of the chair, toppling it over, as she moved to the lantern on the table. Metal grated on metal as she pried off the fuel valve, then poured some of the grain alcohol on to the tattered duvet. Returning the lantern to the table, Maizy retrieved the broken match box and one unbroken matchstick.

Fuel vapors whooshed when Maizy dropped the lit match on the eiderdown quilt; flames licked the surface of the feather-filled bedspread then dipped into its depths where some of the fuel had saturated. Shadows lifted off the floor and waltzed across the walls as fire blazed from the ruined duvet. Maizy took a step back, the heat drying the tears on her face.

Maizy looked down at her hands, flexing her fingers. Smudges of dirt and soot darkened her skin, her flesh split in several places and showing the redness of infection. Was I capable of doing this, she asked herself. Could everything that I learned throughout my life be cast away and replaced with such a careless means of survival?

Smoke billowed up, thick and hot, roiling across the ceiling in a lake of poisonous vapors. Maizy flung the front door open, letting the low-hanging dark cloud spill out into the night.

The smoke began to thin, yet the fire spread to the overturned chair, engulfing the age-worn wood. Maizy kicked at its upturned legs, sending flaming pieces skittering across the floor. She gagged and spat hot bile into the fire, before being engaged by a fit of coughing. Maizy finally fled to the front door and let the cool night air bathe over her. Hand braced against the door frame, she watched the eiderdown quilt begin to disintegrate into ashes, until her attention was drawn to the rear of the room.

A large crow stood atop Benjamin's bed, its eyes two large black pearls. From its beak hung the torn fragment of wedding dress Maizy had found earlier in the evening. The sight of the bird infuriated Maizy, yet also filled her with fear. Maizy quickly moved to the table and picked up the cigar box containing her sewing materials. Heaving it at the crow, she watched it turn end over end, before it struck the crow and exploded in an array of thread spools and needles.

The bird's great wings flapped, the crow taking to the air and sweeping across the room, before it crashed into the lantern atop the table. Glass shattered, shards reflecting the glow of the fire. Lantern fuel sprayed across the floor, feeding the dying flames. The crow took flight, once again, the strip of wedding dress falling from its beak and into the fire, before it dodged past Maizy and into the night.

Fire spread across the floor, engulfing the room. Maizy stumbled through the doorway, casting a quick glance over her shoulder to see Benjamin's bed disappear behind a wall of fire.

Lightning illuminated the sky; a rumble of thunder following shortly after. Shadows moved about Maizy, the darkness churned by the light cast off by the fire. An owl hooted, its call triggering a cacophony of sounds. And beyond the roaring of the fire and the songs of Mother Nature, Maizy paused as a child's soft singing reached her ears.

Maizy rushed towards the rear of the house, the light from the fire drifting amongst the overgrown foliage. Her feet sunk into the earth, the mud hindering her movement.

She had to find Benjamin. She cast away all thoughts about the previous day and trudged forward, branches snagging in her hair. As the undergrowth became denser, darkness ebbed away the light cast from the fire behind her. The woods seemed to come to life. Creatures moved within the shadows, scampering over wet leaves. Lightning streaked across the sky, illuminating hunched figures in the undergrowth, betrayed by their glowing eyes.

Maizy stopped beneath a great oak, listening to the lullaby that drifted to her midst the resonant forest.

And momma said it's time for bed, before the sun drifts o'er the mornin'.

Fatigue chased her, but Maizy rushed forward, her hands batting away hanging vines and impeding branches. The trees parted before her as she found easier footing and stumbled into a small clearing. Her eyes adjusted to the dim light as she continued forward, knowing that each step drew her closer to an answer, with questions she dared not ask.

Wings beat the air above her. Maizy ducked low and covered her head, all the while moving away from the shelter of the trees. Something flew by, inches away from her, as she quickened her pace.

Then time stood still, Maizy's foot caught midair. She balanced on the threshold of the well, realization twining about her frail body. She closed her eyes, weightless for a single moment, before she lost all balance and fell forward into darkness.

Her head glanced off the lip of the well, the corroded brick tearing flesh from Maizy's scalp. Her body became that of a ragdoll, toppled a hundred feet into the ground, where the walls drew blood and the final impact shattered bone. Shadows caressed Maizy, while streams of water wept down moss-covered stone. A spider skittered away, abandoning its newly spun web.

Searing pain rocked Maizy into consciousness, pushing her towards madness. A sliver of moon cast light down into the well, illuminating her left arm, which bent backwards at the elbow, a spike of ivory protruding between crimson lips of skin. When she tried to move her legs, broken bone scraped against broken bone, the carnage hidden beneath the wells murky water. She took a deep breath, then exhaled, her throat making a gurgling sound as blood seeped into a punctured lung, then filled the back of her throat. She coughed and spat.

Maizy looked up towards the mouth of the well, her eyes adjusting to the dim light. An amber glow shimmered over the lip of the well, telling her that the fire still burned the remnants of the house. She then cast her eyes about the bottom of the well. Maizy noticed the shaft of the well narrowed to an area no more than five feet around. A break in the wall led into a dark void in front of her, her legs lying partially in its shadow. Water sloshed, loosening gravel from the lining of the aquifer as Maizy tried to pull her legs from the half-submerged channel.

The walls echoed movement from within the shadows. Maizy choked back a scream and tried to push herself back against the cold rock behind her. The joint in her right shoulder popped, the pain halting her movement. She panted, coughed and began to whimper quietly.

A small hand slithered over the crumbling wall, the flesh pale and stained with grime. Another hand whispered over her broken legs, before finding purchase on the opposite wall. When Benjamin broke into the light, Maizy squeezed her eyes shut, trying to block out the haunting black orbs which stared out from behind drifting locks of hair. The stench of death filled Maizy's nostrils, coupled with the scent of damp earth.

Finally, she forced herself to look upon her dead son.

"I didn't mean to", Maizy cried

Benjamin drew closer and crouched before her, his jaw moving slowly as bone grated behind a torn cheek.

"*Momma, don't cry.*" Benjamin's voice was filled with water. "*All I ever wanted to do was make you happy.*"

Maizy lifted her hand and stroked his hair.

"*How about if I sing to you?*"

Maizy nodded and laid her head back against the wall, a final tear coursing down her cheek.

"I think I'd like that," she said and let her eyes drift shut.

With a penchant for graveyard photography and necro-tourism trips around his home state of Michigan, **Mark A. France** still sleeps with his baby blanket and avoids looking out the back window of his bedroom late at night, for fear that he may see something moving amongst the shadows. Yet, these fears play heavily into his writing, which often focus on macabre tales woven with the patchwork of the human condition. From ghosts to corpses raised from the grave, **France** takes simple situations and laces them with complex characters in terrifying settings, brought to life by his unique style of writing. France is also an avid photographer and award-winning filmmaker.

Survivalist Mountain

Benjamin T. Smith

There were once two brothers, one rich and the other poor. The rich one had moved away from the family farm as a young adult, earning his wealth in the great city, the financial capital of the world. He cared nothing for the poor brother, who had chosen to maintain their parents' traditions and till the land. He had greater ambitions, choosing instead to till the finances and treasuries of the people.

Life was often hard for the poor brother. The land was afflicted by drought more often than not, forcing him to use genetically modified crops that were heartier and more drought resistant than their natural counterparts, but which did not give up usable seeds of their own.

In addition to this, he and his neighbors had given up growing wheat and other foods for human consumption in favor of corn to be used in the production of biofuels. The guaranteed ethanol subsidies had allowed the community to prosper modestly for many years until the second drought — a financial one — descended upon the land.

This drought — later known as the Great Collapse — was far worse than any weather-borne calamity. As one the global financial markets — built entirely upon debt and backed by no tangible assets — crashed into utter ruin, bringing down the societies dependent upon them. All the world was taken by surprise, though it had been long in the making and numerous in its signs and portents.

The poor brother had watched in horror as — overnight — the savings he and his wife had spent years accumulating vanished into complete worthlessness. Even had the banks not declared an indefinite holiday he could not have afforded a single loaf of bread with what was in his account, such was the extent of the currency's devaluation. Not that any store near him would have had any food. The grocery store and bakery had been ransacked in a matter of hours by panicked neighbors and townsmen, who suddenly realized they might never again have another chance to stock their pantries.

He and his fellow farmers now cursed themselves for selling their corn crop in the days before the Great Collapse, for now all they had were empty fields and wallets full of worthless paper. The scrips of currency might serve as kindling for a hearthfire, but it would do little to fill their bellies.

His wife had maintained a garden, and so they had some vegetables on hand at summer's end. The canning equipment had sat unused since his mother's time, but they soon dusted it off along with as many jars as they could find, and set to work canning whatever they could not immediately consume. Between that and what remained in their pantry, it would have to do.

It was not enough. It could not be enough, not with as many children as the pair of them had. Worse still were the prospects of spring and what meager harvest they could hope to bring with the few seeds they had on hand.

Once winter arrived he took to the woods with a rifle in order to hunt for deer and other wild game. He had some success with this, although animals quickly became scarce due to his neighbors and many from nearby towns coming out to do the same. This required him to venture further and further away from his farm to hunt.

While he was walking along a goat trail one day he heard something he had not heard in months: the sound of a diesel engine! It sounded as if it was coming up the trail. Nervous, he shouldered his rifle and climbed up into a nearby evergreen tree. Soon he was up on a high branch, giving him a good view of his surroundings.

Directly in front of him was a large hill he had never seen before! He had been a teenager when the government had restricted access to this area, so it had been years since he had walked this trail. Where had this mountain of a hill come from?

The sound of the engine grew louder, and before long a large diesel truck pulled up next to a vine-covered portion of the hill. Four men—each wearing body armor and with a carbine slung across his chest—alighted from the vehicle. Three surveyed the woodland around them while one, the driver, began pulling the vines away, as if they covered something.

The poor brother was intrigued at what he was seeing. He leaned cross the branch he was resting on and used the scope of his rifle to watch the man working at the vines. The sun was at his back, so he did not fear any gleam from his lens giving away his position to the other three.

The driver cleared enough of the vines away to reveal a large keypad. He slowly punched in four digits, as if he were afraid of getting the combination wrong. Immediately a large doorway opened up in the side of the hill, revealing a dimly lit corridor within. The four quickly disappeared inside, the doorway closing up behind them.

Several minutes went by, and many times the man in the tree had to remind himself to breathe. Despite the chill he could himself growing sweaty from nervousness.

Finally the door opened again and the four men trundled out, each carrying a heavy crate. In short order they had the back of the truck loaded down. The three clambered back into their seats while the driver punched the same code into the keypad to get the door to close. He then camouflaged it with the vines once more before returning to his seat and starting up the engine.

The man waited until the sound of the engine had faded into the distance before climbing down from the tree. He crept up to the hillside and cleared away the vines from the keypad. He then punched in the four numbers he had seen the other one use: one-seven-nine-one.

The door opened and he stepped inside. It was a government bunker! All along the corridor he saw crates of goods, many unopened. Several doorways led to more storage chambers, and each was filled with all manner of supplies: freeze-dried and dehydrated food, medical supplies, seed packets, water treatment equipment, and portable light sources.

He had brought a pack large enough to carry over a hundred pounds of venison had his hunt been successful, and this he filled with food, antibiotics, seeds, and a couple of small solar lanterns for the farmhouse. He did his best to disturb as little as possible, so that his presence would remain a secret.

He even found a small room filled with gold and silver bouillon. This he left alone, both out of fear of those who had been here before and also because he knew it would serve no practical purpose. His wife and children could not eat gold, and neither could any of his neighbors.

At the start of the Great Collapse six months ago, he might have been tempted, considering how distraught he was over the loss of his family's savings. Now he realized that precious metals, like paper money, were not so precious when no one was willing to trade for it.

He closed up the entrance and covered it with vines before heading back for home, making sure to cover his tracks until he was back onto the goat trail. It would not do for those men to discover he had been there and then follow him home, after all.

His wife was ecstatic when he returned home that evening and showed her what his pack was filled with. "This will be enough to get us through summer, surely!" she had exclaimed. He knew better. The amount he could carry in one trip would barely be enough for a couple of months, but it would help augment what they already had.

The supplies did not last them even a month. His neighbors were suffering as much as they, some more so. Compassion filled their hearts, and little by little they shared what they had with their neighbors, knowing full well that the entire community had to survive the winter if any of them were to have a chance. Soon the food and the medicine were gone.

The man returned to the hillside bunker once more and loaded the pack down with more of what he had taken the last time: food, medical supplies, seeds, and lanterns. Once more he did not touch any of the gold and silver.

Shortly after returning this second time the man's rich brother arrived at the farm. His fine clothes were threadbare, and the story he told of the great city was one of chaos, violence, and despair. He and his companions had been fine for a time, protected as they were by armed guards.

Eventually the food had run out, and the guards had left to tend to their own families. He had soon fled the city with naught but the clothes on his back. He had left all his wealth and status behind, and it ate away at him.

The poor brother welcomed him as the father of the prodigal son had, and this had only rankled his once-rich brother. What galled him even more was how generous the poor brother was with what he had. The once-rich brother had jealously guarded everything he had earned, and he had earned quite a bit! And here was his poor, dirt farming brother—a man who could never hope to make the kind of money he had once made—giving away what he had to help his neighbors. It was little wonder he was as poor as he was, if this was where his sensibilities lay!

And yet, the once-rich brother could not help but wonder where some of these goods were coming from. He had not spent much time in the cellar, yet it seemed strange that they would have so many seeds and lanterns to give out to others.

The poor brother's secret was discovered the third time he ventured into the bunker for more food for his family and neighbors. His once-rich brother was waiting for him when he arrived home. Before the poor farmer could stop him his brother had pulled the pack from his shoulders and was rifling through it. The once-rich brother demanded to know where he had gotten this from, and what else was there. The poor brother, taken aback by this verbal assault, told everything. He even mentioned the gold and silver he had seen there, and the passcode for getting in: one-seven-nine-one.

The once-rich brother immediately dumped the contents of his poor brother's pack all over the ground. He then shouldered the pack and made off for the hill without looking back. He, too, remembered the goat trail from his youth, and would have no problem finding it.

When he came to the hill he cleared away the vines and entered the code his brother had given him: one-seven-nine-one. The door opened just as his brother had said it would. Satisfied, he entered and let the door close behind him. He looked around and saw the same supplies his brother had been collecting, only he looked upon these with disgust. "Where are the valuables?" he growled as he tore through boxes and threw their contents around.

Eventually he came to the room with the gold and silver bouillon, and he began loading the pack down with as much as he could carry. He could barely contain his glee. This was it! This would help him rebuild his fortune!

Once the backpack was filled and he tried to leave he discovered he could not remember the door code! He had been so consumed with his own greed that everything else had left his mind. Was it one-seven-seven-six? Or maybe one-eight-one-two? It was some date significant in his country's history, but he had never paid any mind to such things before now.

As each code he entered proved to be invalid he grew more and more panicked. How was he going to get out of here?

Suddenly the door opened, and not by his doing. He backed away from the now open portal as one man entered followed by three more. All four were armed with rifles that they quickly leveled at his chest.

The straps on his overburdened pack chose that moment to break. With a crash the pack struck the floor and burst at the seams, scattering gold and silver across the corridor.

"We finally caught you," one of the men said. "We've seen you here before, and each time we could find nothing other than necessities missing, and that we could let slide. Times are hard for everyone." He glanced down at the precious metals lying at the once-rich brother's feet and said, "I guess this finally proved to be too tempting a target, eh?"

"You've got the wrong man!" the once-rich brother pleaded. "That was my fool brother those other times! This is my first time here!"

"Your brother?" the man said. "Well, that would explain the sudden change in habits. Your brother's a more sensible man than you."

"He's also about to be more alive than you," one of the others said as each man turned their rifle safeties off with an audible click.

ᘿᘩᘓ

When Benjamin T. Smith *is not writing fantasy and science fiction he is reading or irritating his wife with story ideas. He has previously been published in* Kaleidotrope *and* Voluted Tales *ezines, anthologies for* Chaosium *and* Fringeworks, *and he received an honorable mention for an entry to the* In Places Between *contest of 2013. Ben is currently working on several short stories and even a novel or two. He lives out in the middle of rural America with his wife, their collection of anime and books, and their garden. Keep up with him at Benjamintsmith.net. When he decides to post, that is!*

Death's Messengers

Jason Barney

Rudy was jogging.

The early weeks of summer were well past, and now the true heat had arrived The leaves were flush and green, reaching upwards in anticipation of the next passing shower or thunderstorm. The days were long so he ran in the morning. It was unhealthy for physical activity in the ninety degree July afternoons.

Just out of high school and rarely having listened to his teachers, Rudy had retained only a desire to stay in shape from any of his classes. Gym had made sense.

The novels the English teacher's assigned sucked.

He hated math.

The history department was as archaic as the shit they made the students read about.

And science, who the hell needed that?

Keeping in shape, he understood that.

The aches and strains of his muscles felt good. There was discomfort, but it was the limited pain an athletic body wanted. His calves and thighs buzzed with fatigue. They were starting to feel hot, as though the inside of his legs was getting too close to a flame. He loved the air moving in and out of his lungs. He was running at a pretty good clip. He was sweating profusely and looked like he had just gotten out of the shower.

It was while contemplating his physical activity that Rudy came across the old man.

At some point in the last several years, the local governments had converted the old railroad beds into bike paths. He had been over them since childhood. Sometimes exercising, often walking with friends. It was as familiar to him as the road a family takes to church on a Sunday morning.

Except large boulders had never blocked the path just north of the Missisquoi River. The area was fairly remote. A few stretches of the trail ran along sharp walls of rock, where the railroad companies had dynamited a century and a half ago.

Rudy slowed his pace and reached for his MP3 player's ear phones. He liked to jog with AC/DC smashing in his head.

The bike path was nearly impassable.

Boulders the size of pickup trucks blocked his route. A large gaping hole was in the rock face above the old rail trail. It looked like the top of some ancient volcano. Rudy thought of the thunderstorm last evening. It had been quite active, lightning like a thousand cameras at a large sporting event. The winds had been insane.

His speed decreased to a walk. Then he heard the moaning.

At first he wasn't sure what it was. It could have been the engine of some vehicle zooming by in the distance. As his mind connected the dots he stepped toward the boulders, disbelieving there could be anyone alive under all of that disarray.

His heart went from physical exertion to nervous beating as reality set in. Someone was trapped in there, probably crushed, but still alive. He suddenly felt cold, as though he had stepped outside on a late October morning. The moans were louder. Whoever was inside that mess was experiencing more than pain. Coughing, shrieking, bellowing. It sounded like a wounded dog. The eerie sounds echoed off what remained of the hillside.

Rudy weaved between two massive rocks, and hopped up on a third. By the time he was twenty or so feet off the ground, he realized he was the only potential rescuer around. He cursed himself for not paying attention during the First Aid section of health class.

His eyes found the victim of the rockslide.

A very mangled body, wearing black, was at the bottom of a deep crevice formed by the fallen boulders. The person's legs were crushed. Rudy had the odd thought his weight was pushing down harder on the victim so he shifted to another ledge. He recoiled when he saw a full view of the trapped individual.

The body just ended where the rocks began. It looked like an illusion a magician might pull off. The clothing seemed out of place, very much like a cloak. The person's back was covered with dust and dirt.

A microwave oven sized rock rested on his right shoulder. The arms where outstretched as though sliding headfirst into home plate. Long gray, mangy hair, like that of a cat that has never been taken care of, tangled out from a skull that lay crooked against the ground. It was thin enough where Rudy saw rounded, wrinkly scalp. He immediately thought of his ninety-five year old grandmother, and wondered how someone so old could have been out on the bike path in the first place.

The person let out a hollow shriek.

Rudy looked around, back down the bike path, desperate for help.

When the man's arms started flailing as if he was trying to swim, Rudy knew he had to try to help. It was impossible that the ancient looking man was still alive, but there he was.

Rudy descended over rubble, several feet closer. Dust and dirt caked his sweaty hands and forearms. Jagged edges and sharp sections jutted out like broken glass.

It was when Rudy went down another five or six feet, almost to within reach of the guy, when he froze. He had been having the thought that he needed to call 911 but he didn't have his cell. His feet delicately balanced on a long, unsteady stretch of rock, like a surfer riding a wave.

The man tried to lift his head. The skin on the dirty face was pruned similar to hands in water for too long. His lips were bulging and gray. The mouth was absent of half of its teeth, giving the odd appearance of a rotting jack-o-lantern. The skin around the cheeks was flaky and bruised. Rudy saw unimaginable agony on the old man's face. It was every description of childbirth he'd ever heard, multiplied by ten.

And then the man saw him.

It wasn't something Rudy expected. Somehow those roaming eyes, the face dealing with all of that pain, found him.

Even if Rudy had made up his mind to drop down further, he doubted he could have. The eyes were brownish yellow, close to the color of fried eggs. Wrinkling skin pulled away from both sockets. The eyeballs protruded out of his face, like the top of two turnips in a garden. Bloody jagged streaks of red surrounded each pupil.

Then he noticed the smell.

It immediately reminded him of stale cigarette smoke and aging grandparents. He had a memory of his grandfather's poorly shaved stubble running along his own cheeks and his grandmother's sagging face.

As his eyes locked with the old man's, a vision started. He was mind was instantly somewhere else. It was like two people, phones raised in the air, searching for the best cell phone reception. When contact was made, Rudy's mind started receiving.

His body remained perched, feet above the carnage, but he saw what the old man was.

Death.

Waves of identifiers seeped into his consciousness. This man, this thing... had stalked the wounded on every battlefield through time. Men in armor with hacked off limbs. Bullet wounds; this entity had visited each of them. It had called upon every natural disaster the world had ever known and helped spread every deadly disease. Rudy saw people dying of immense coughing fits, bodies sweating, eating themselves out from the inside.

Rudy threw up.

The bile leapt from his stomach and stormed up his throat. It was almost a relief. He didn't know how much his psyche could take. In front of him, in human form, was the definition finality.

He gasped for air. He was still sweating and cold, as though he'd been jogging in the middle of the winter.

The vision intensified and he swayed. For an instant, he believed he would fall, the way a bowling pin rolls and teeters just before toppling over. His hand steadied against solid rock.

Despite his failing balance, his eyes remained in Death's grip.

And he saw what had happened.

Even Death had enemies.

On the plain of some distant realm, in a world where giants existed, Death had somehow lost one of his campaigns for a soul. Rudy saw a hulk of a man, perhaps as tall as a telephone pole and as well muscled as a body builder, walking along a well traveled path. Patches of grass pushed out from either side, the soil bare and exposed from constant travel. The giant's skin was glacier blue, he wore animal furs over his chest and waist.

In his hands was a little blue baby. The giant cradled it, hugged it, held it up in outstretched arms to laughter and smiles. Rudy wondered if it would grow as large as its father.

Old man Death appeared from the tall grass, the same frail entity which lay buried beneath rock in his world. The robe was black and flowing. His shoulders were hunched, the head almost falling forward, scraggily hair ejecting out in all directions.

Rudy's heart pounded so hard he wondered if he were having a heart attack.

Death approached the giant, arms up, motioning for the baby.

The most incredible altercation ensued.

The giant knelt close to the ground as the darkness approached. Death was energized by the opportunity to seize the child. He leaned forward, fingers within a few feet of the little one.

Closed fists pounded down on the head and shoulders of the old man. The giant's fist was easily twice size of Death's head. The blows came down like the boulder hitting the Wily Coyote in the children's cartoon. But Death's eyes never left the child, and this enraged the giant more. Kicks capable of breaking bones impacted against the old man's midsection. He was pummeled, as a bully might beat a child.

At first there was little physical evidence the beating was having any effect. Death was thrown around, but he was able to stand after each blow, able to step toward the baby. When the blue skinned beast ripped up a tree trunk used it as a club, things got bad.

Bruises formed on Death's head where impacts were intended to crush his skull. Saggy skin separated, and gray brown puss emerged. Rudy wondered if death were bleeding. After several blows, the old man could no longer move.

If the child had been any older, it would have witnessed a raw experience about life. The infant was on the ground, however, its head angled up, tiny fingers grasping at clouds. Its father flailed away, like a criminal assaulting a victim. Sweat poured from his body. His muscles bulged. And he beat the living snot out of Death.

The encounter ended when Death tried to stand, but could not. He saw the giant coming, and raised his arms to protect his face.

The giant pulled back his club the way a baseball player gets ready for a pitch. And then, at the instant Rudy thought he would see a swing....Death was gone. It took him a moment to realize the giant had indeed swung, that his full wrath had been unleashed.

Loud thunder clapped from the skies and echoed across the horizon.

And the blue baby started to cry.

The vision ended. The world shifted. Rudy sagged against the closest rock. A heavy layer of dirt caked onto his soaked clothing. He felt so tired he wondered if he were about to pass out. He was concealed from the rest of the world, atop a precipice, looking into the eyes of a being everyone hated. For the first time in his life, Rudy truly felt fear.

He had to get away before death took him. The Reaper was injured, having retreated from the realm of the giant and ending up here. The taker of souls hadn't come for him, but would if given the chance.

Rudy swallowed. Death's eyes bore into him. He felt himself starting to float.

His knees weakened. Death's aurora was similar to a moth flying toward flame. Rudy used the ledge as support. He pulled his eyes away and looked up and out of the pit. Gray skies greeted him.

"Wait," a coughing, whispery voice said. "Please...."

Rudy started climbing out. Pebbles rolled from under his shoes and fell below. He didn't care if he caused an avalanche. Rudy let panic take him, like a deer bolting away from a hunter.

"I....have....not....come...for....you...," Death sobbed.

For a moment, Rudy hesitated. Concepts of religion ran through his mind. He saw spring unfolding on bright, warm days; winter coming in on soft unforgiving snowflakes. All he had been raised to know had been challenged. His mind accepted, for a fleeting moment, that the ancient robbed creature was indeed the taker of life. His consciousness understood there were other realms of giants, elves, spirits, and dragons.

In a heartbeat, in order to keep him sane, his ego rejected those realities. It was like the natural reflex of pulling a hand away from a scorching hot stove.

"I...beg...you..." Death cried.

Rudy reached the top. His forearms and wrists burned with exhaustion, his legs cramped. He leapt down, away from the old man, and didn't look back. Like a bird in flight he was gone. And Death lay there, injured, near the end.

✿

Sixty-one years passed. Rudy Stanford lived a fairly normal life. He moved away from Franklin County, Vermont three times. He stayed away for nearly ten years during one stretch. Twice he married. His first wife left him after five years. There were two kids from that relationship. Late in his thirties he remarried, and had two more children. He remained with his second wife for most of his life.

By the time he was in his early sixties, there were three grandchildren. When he reached his seventies there were six. People were having kids later in life nowadays.

When absent from Vermont he felt restless, like someone trying to sleep on an unfamiliar mattress. The green mountain state always called to him. The four seasons defined life. Rudy loved white Christmases with family and grilling hot dogs and hamburgers under the steamy July sun.

As youth turned to middle age and then middle age bled into retirement, Rudy detected the signs of change along the way. The beard hairs on his chin were salt and pepper gray by the time he was thirty. At forty he complained to friends how painful it was to stretch, how difficult it was to jog. In his early fifties he'd dealt with skin cancer on one ear. His sixties brought a bulging belly and thinning hair. By his seventh and eighth decades Rudy Stanford was in fact elderly, but in surprisingly good shape. His blood pressure was fine, he didn't smoke, and he visited the doctor as he should.

But time was winning. The decades had slipped by. He did not recall things easily anymore. It was as though all his memories were dreams from the previous night's sleep. Each evening he forgot more of them, each day, his mind got a little foggier.

It was on a late July evening, when Rudy Stanford truly comprehended life and death. Every action has an equal and opposite reaction and he was now an old man.

❦

He sat in the recliner, straining not to shift his weight for the hundredth time. His thighs were cramping, his legs felt like they were an old cushion that needed to be replaced. His muscles were always like that.

Sarah Mae, the first of his great grandchildren, sat on his lap, holding the book full of Grimm's Fairy tales. She was five years old, her little frame the size of elves and dwarves that showed up in so many make believe stories. She wore a little yellow dress like Cinderella, and Rudy thought her hair was as beautiful.

The rest of the family was around the house. Some of his children, now themselves pushing sixty, were either on the porch dealing with their own fatigue or were conversing in the kitchen. A few of them were sipping beer, helping to take a little bit of the pain out of life. Not all the grandchildren were present, but a few of them, now adults, tended the fire pit out back.

Which left Great Grandpa Rudy alone, struggling to balance little Sarah Mae. They were in his rocking chair, something he enjoyed from his youth, a memory that always fit perfectly, like old leather.

It was a physical struggle to balance the child and deal with the constant aches and pains that ravaged his body. The young didn't know what it was like. How it was difficult to just hold onto a child. Sometimes getting up from a chair was difficult. Rudy wished he would have been able to put some of his youth in a jar and save it. He wasn't in a wheel chair, and his kids hadn't considered the nursing home option-yet. But the end of his life was approaching, and he knew it.

Everyone did.

His shoulders were always hunched, his neck didn't hold his head up anymore, only out, as though he were always trying to smell something. He still had good use of his fingers, but he discovered the definition of arthritis long ago.

"You choose one," she said, fumbling through the fairy tale book. It had a colorful cover, as though the artist had captured all of the shades and hues in a flower garden. It was hard bound, which Rudy liked.

"Great Grandpa...." Sarah Mae said, going through the pages. She started to kick her feet and lean back and forth, wanting to rock.

"Hold your horses," Rudy teased, tickling her. "Let an old man go at his own pace."

"Chose one," she ordered, oblivious to everything in the world except her great grandfather, and the attention she was receiving.

"Hhhmmmm, let me see," he said. She cuddled up to him.

There was a knock at the door. Rudy wondered if more of the family had shown up. Someone yelled they would get it. He was looking forward to joining them outside. He could already smell the hamburgers and hotdogs on the fire.

Rudy's fingers flipped through the pages, more unique artwork catching his eye. He wondered how old the book was. The horses literally came out at you. The old bridges were magnificent and detailed. Castles were full and impressive, the forest settings seemed real.

"What about this one?" Rudy asked.

"What is it about?" the eager little girl asked, looking more at him than the book.

Rudy froze.

A form he had not seen in a lifetime was splayed on the page. He remembered the robe. He tried to shift Sarah Mae, so that he could bring the open book closer, like a librarian searching for a blemish in an old collection. His arms wouldn't move.

His eyes still could, and they searched the paper.

Grimm's Fairy Tale # 177

Death's Messengers

Rudy felt cold, as though it was the middle of December and someone had left the front door open. He tried to reposition himself again, to shift Sarah Mae, but the only part of his body working correctly seemed to be his eyes. He blinked, felt the air going in and out of his lungs, but everything else was caught in cement.

"You are having a stroke," said a voice he had not heard in generations. It came from down the hall, near the front door.

The book. It was still open. The fairy tale of Death's Messengers was still there.

"I have been keeping tabs on you, my old friend," said the voice. It was moving, floating, getting closer. It was him.

There, on page 177, was the same being he had refused to help sixty some odd years ago. Rudy remembered the crushed form, the bones that had to have been broken. He recalled the awful face, the vision that tested his sanity.

"No," the voice said, "That was real, and you damn well know it."

Three thoughts crept into Rudy's mind. The first was that Sarah Mae wasn't moving, her little body was stuck, balancing on his leg. The second was that he was scared, for the vision had tormented his dreams. Lastly, Rudy understood he was dying.

"Very good, my old friend," Death said from the hall. The voice was like low sounding bursts of music coming from a very old church organ.

Death limped around the corner of the room. The robe was tattered and oily. Its hood was drawn over a shriveled skull and wrinkled face. He used a long piece of black wood as a walking staff.

"My family?" Rudy was surprised to hear his own voice.

"Oh, I think you already know that answer to that," Death said. There was a flash, as though a lightning strike had brightened a dark room, and visions seeped into his mind. Rudy saw his visitors collapsed on chairs, slumped in unlikely positions. Hands clutched hearts. Fingers and palms held skulls. Hands clenched stomachs. Some members of his family just seemed to be locked in time. They were unmoving, fastened in whatever they had been doing.

Rudy's heart beat quickly, wondering if some of them might survive.

"I am not done, yet." Death said.

"The children?" Rudy managed, shocked that his ability to speak was still there.

"Don't get your hopes up."

Rudy's heart pounded in his chest. Despite his inability to move, his eyes were damp.

"There…there…yes, that's it….get it all out," the demon mocked.

"Why my family?" Rudy managed.

"If it needs explaining, dear boy," the Reaper said, "I'll simply say this. I come for countless people each day. I get up in the morning, like everyone else. Have a cup of coffee. I go to work. Sometimes I just plod through the hours, taking the souls I'm supposed to. You know how a job feels sometimes."

Rudy sensed Death was enjoying this.

"There are special events, though. Days when the unexpected happens. They add a bit of a thrill, really." For an instant, there was pain on Death's face, and then it was gone. "My encounter with that Giant and his child? That pretty much sucked. But in the end, they got what they had coming, I assure you. I always get my man."

Death inched up to him, like a senior citizen in a nursing home. The hood shadowed that horrid face. Rudy smelled a revolting combination of dead fish, rotting veggies, and shit.

"On that day, years ago, when you ran from me….I noticed you, sir."

Rudy understood. It was as simple as the moon rising against the horizon, as normal as the sun setting each evening. Rains came and went. Death had noticed him.

The hooded being's head dropped to the book. He was smiling.

"Just so you know, I played by the rules, I sent you my messengers."

Rudy didn't understand.

"Oh poor thing," Death said. "That's right. You don't know the Fairy Tale of Death's Messengers? I sent you pain in your joints, that quick bout with cancer, the gray hair, the wrinkles….I gave you plenty of warnings."

"Do you have to take my family, too?" Rudy managed. A tear dropped from his cheek.

In desperation, Rudy hoped some ancient religious faith, a belief in heaven, God, or angels would come and save his loved ones.

The world started to go black.

"Yes," said Death, coughing. "I'm taking your family, too"

Jason Barney *lives in Vermont. He is 38 years old and teaches high school social studies. He doesn't get the opportunity to write as much as he would like, but truly enjoys it when he gets the chance. He can be contacted at ad-miralriker_jay@yahoo.com.*

The Golden Key

Wendy Nikel

"What do you think happened to him?"

Detective Reginald Helms scowled, biting the end of his pencil. He hadn't been on the crime scene more than three minutes, yet this rookie cop — little more than a crossing guard, really — thought that because he had "detective" on his name tag that he was some sort of modern-day Sherlock Holmes. How many times did he have to put up with the same unoriginal jokes or remind people that it was "Helms" not "Holmes." It almost made him want to legally change his name. Or quit the force. It hadn't been nearly so bad until they started showing all those TV crime scene dramas, where they manage to solve the case and lock away the bad guy in the time it takes the viewer to chow down a bag of Doritos. Maybe he should consider an early retirement.

"Won't know much till we get the autopsy back," he said to deflect the question. He bent down in the dingy slush to study the victim. Hours ago, this path through the woods must have been completely obscured by the new snowfall. Over a foot had fallen overnight, but by the time Helms arrived on the scene, any that the sun hadn't already melted had been stomped down into a dirty, icy-brown muck, first by the searchers, and later by the gawkers, until finally police officers that had roped off the scene and forced the nosy onlookers back to their regularly scheduled day among the living.

As for Helms, his day would be spent with the recently deceased. The victim was male, late teens or early twenties, about 6' tall and around 180 lbs. He was wearing jeans and a hooded sweatshirt from the nearby college. Or at least it had been a sweatshirt. Now it was little more than scarlet ribbons strewn like streamers across his chest. The detective, despite his years of seeing much worse injuries than this, still cringed at the sight.

"Must've been a wild animal," the rookie said with wide eyes.

Helms sighed. "And what makes you think that, boy?"

The stringy cop turned bright red and stuttered a bit before finally spitting out, "Well, the bite and scratch marks on the victim... I thought..."

The red gashes across the victim's chest and arms certainly seemed to indicate that.

"Have you gotten any wild animal reports in this area recently?" Helms asked, pushing his glasses up on his nose.

"Well... no."

"Which way do you think this vicious, hypothetical wild animal went?"

"Well, um..." The rookie turned around in a circle, searching the ground for a trail of paw prints. Helms, though, was a couple steps ahead of him already.

"There are no prints," he said with a sweeping gesture of his arm. "Nor are there any tufts of fur like one would expect to find with a wild animal attack."

"Does that mean... what happened?"

"Well, boy," Helms said grimly, "that's what we're here to find out. Now if you'll quit yammering for ten seconds, maybe I'll be able to do my work."

A moment of silence passed between them. The rookie stood, shifting from one foot to another in a way that reminded Helms of a metronome. He pretended not to notice, but the constant motion chafed his calm.

"Oh, I almost forgot." The rookie snapped his fingers. He dug into his jacket pocket and pulled out a small, spiral-bound notebook. "Here are the notes from the interviews, sir."

The detective didn't even look up as he reached out a hand to take the notes. He flipped through the pages, trying to connect the dots. Each case was like one of those newspaper number puzzles—Suki, or Sudako, or whatever they were called. Everything had to line up perfectly: the means, the motive, the opportunity, or else the whole puzzle was wrong and you might as well ball it up and throw it in the trash bin. Unless you used pencil, of course. Helms never used pencil. He made sure things lined up correctly the first time.

"According to roommates, the victim left his dorm at around 11:30 p.m. to go to the Quick-E-Mart for some soda pop," the rookie recited, reading over Helms' shoulder.

Helms patted down the victim's pockets. In one of the jacket pockets, he came across a wallet. The detective pulled out two drivers' licenses. The same smiling face peered out from both, but the birthdates indicated were two years apart.

"Make a note to check with the clerk whether Mr. Andrew Westshore here has made any 'soda pop' purchases in the past," Helms said, tossing the wallet over his shoulder. The rookie fumbled it, and it fell to the ground. He picked it up and searched the other compartments, but only found a student ID, a debit card, and a twenty dollar bill.

"The convenience store clerk did recognize the vic's photo from previous visits, but said that he hadn't seen him last night." The rookie shrugged. "I guess the vic never made it."

"Or the witness is lying," Helms muttered. The point of his pen never touched one of those Japanese number-box puzzle squares unless he knew for sure which digit belonged there. He looked up and squinted through the trees. From this narrow stretch of woods, one could just barely make out the flickering neon sign of the Quick-E-Mart in one direction. In the opposite direction, the gray stone of the college dorms were more difficult to see, but the detective knew there was less than two miles between the two, if you cut through these woods.

The rookie watched him surveying the distance. "Would've thought that someone would have seen something, huh?"

Helms frowned at the intrusion on his thoughts, and refused to look up at the scrawny cop. "Visibility last night around 11:30 was less than three feet. The kid could have gotten lost in his own back yard."

"Oh." The rookie flushed and made himself busy flipping through the victim's wallet once more.

There was nothing else in the victim's pockets, but Helms noticed that his hand was clenched tight. Rigor mortis had already begun to set in, so it took some effort for him to pry the object from his palm. When he finally freed it, he held it up to get a better look.

A key.

A tiny, golden key. It was the kind one might expect to use for a grandmother's vintage writing desk—plain and yet beautiful, with a metal loop for the handle, on which one might string a colorful ribbon or a piece of leather to tie around one's neck. The gold glinted in the sun.

Helms stood up to get a better view of the scene. If the victim had the key in his hand, perhaps whatever it was for was nearby, or was somehow related to the murder. Though the path itself was clear, piles of snow still spread all around the body itself. Helms frowned at himself for forgetting his gloves. He could just picture them, sitting on his desk at the office atop his newspaper, needlessly keeping the pages all warm and cozy while his hands were out here freezing. He squinted up into the sky. From his coat, he pulled a copy of the Old Farmers Almanac, and, after flipping through, studying a chart or two, and doing a few calculations, he tucked it back in his coat.

"I'm done with the body, but don't let them move anything else," he said to the officers on duty as he left the scene. "It'll be back in an hour. It'll be easier to see what's really happened here once the snow's melted. Here, hang onto this for me while I go check out the vic's dorm room. You see if there's anything around here it might fit in." *Might as well give him something to do*, Helms thought. *Make him feel useful.*

The rookie nodded solemnly and clutched the key with both hands. Helms just rolled his eyes and let out a huff of breath that made the tiny hairs of his moustache quiver.

When he arrived at the victim's dorm room, a crowd of people had already gathered there as well. He cleared his throat and — like Moses striking his staff upon the waters of the Red Sea — a path opened in front of him.

He walked past the pajama-clad undergrads, who had already littered the hallway outside the victim's room with a memoriam of Glade candles, Facebook photos printed on cheap copy paper, and stuffed animals that, frankly, had seen better days. "We love you, Andy!" the magic-marker posters declared. Helms harrumphed. If they had loved "Andy" so much, they would have offered to go with him to the Quick-E-Mart.

The room itself was typical of such students: a hodgepodge of childhood memories, overflow of current study material, and a distinct lack of cohesion. Over the next hour, Helms sifted through drawers of sports memorabilia, boxes of books whose spines hadn't even been cracked open, and a closet full of band t-shirts, but didn't find anything into which the small key would fit.

Helms was undeterred. In fact, he had suspected as much, for why would the victim have had the key clutched in his hand unless he was planning on using it immediately? Time to go back and see if the rookie had found anything useful. Helms highly doubted it.

Stepping back outside, he checked the sky once more. The sun beamed down on him, and he wiped his forehead with the back of a hand. Already the snow outside the forest had melted. His boots slurped and squished through the mud created from the combination of melted snow and dozens of feet trampling back and forth down the path.

"Well, now, where'd he wander off to?" he muttered as he came upon the deserted crime scene. He stepped under the yellow tape, now able to see the dirt, stone, and tree roots that made up the forest floor. His eyebrows furrowed, however, when he saw that the body had not been removed.

"What—?"

It was not the same body.

Lying face-down in the dirt, still in his rookie blues, was the officer with whom he had just been speaking. The marks on his chest and arms were the exact same as those on the previous victim. Helms stood over him, completely aghast. He pulled a handkerchief from his pocket and wiped his glasses, trying to regain some of his cool, stoic demeanor. This wasn't a simple number puzzle anymore. This wasn't even one of those blasted Rubik's cubes. This was a puzzle he'd never even seen before, that he didn't even know how to start solving.

Helms knelt by the young cop's side and swept over him, looking for any clues. Clenched in his fist was the golden key. The detective pried it from his hand and held it up, just as he had before. Was this a mere coincidence? Had it really been a wild animal attack? If so, where was it now? Or had the rookie uncovered something? Something he shouldn't have? The detective drew his weapon and spun around, clutching the key to his chest as he panted.

"Come out, whatever you are!" he shouted.

The forest was silent.

He stepped back and his eyes raked over the scene once more. Just as he had anticipated, the snow had melted in the warm morning sun. Aside from the tracks of those who had come to work the crime scene, there were no fresh prints in the soft earth. But there, right beside the victim, was a section of soil that looked like it had been recently overturned. Surely that hadn't been like that before. Helms approached it cautiously.

He knelt in the dirt, still clutching the golden key in his sweaty palm. Slowly at first, he brushed away the soil. It fell away easily, and he dug faster. He felt something solid and cold beneath his fingers. Helms pulled away, but his curiosity got the best of him. Gently pushing aside the dirt, he uncovered more and more of the metal object until he could see that it was a box.

Barely two feet square, the box was the same gold color as the key, elaborately decorated with swirls and curlicues. Was this what had caused so much grief? He holstered his weapon in order to get a better grip on the strange object.

He should really call in to report the new victim, he thought as he heaved the box out of the dirt. It was heavy, but not so heavy that he couldn't lift it himself.

He should really radio in for backup, he realized as he turned it over and over in his hands. The gold glinted in the sunlight. Even the box alone was likely worth hundreds, maybe thousands, for the price of the metal.

He should really wait for a team of experts to break open whatever's in the box. It could be dangerous, he considered as he searched for a keyhole. Finally, he found the tiny hole, so small and discreetly placed within the decorative swirls that he would not have seen it had he not been searching for it.

He should really not be out here on his own, he admitted to himself as he inserted the key into the tiny keyhole. The key fit perfectly. With a final worried glance back over at his fallen comrade, the detective turned the key in the lock.

The box sprung open.

The last thing the detective ever saw was rows and rows of sharp, metal teeth, headed straight towards him. His last thought was of the golden key and the numbers of a Sudoku puzzle all falling instantly into place.

❦

When **Wendy Nikel** *is not busy writing about time travel, enchanted islands, or strange creatures, she enjoys taking photographs, playing video games with her husband, and building Lego spaceships with her two sons. Information about her previously published and coming-soon short stories can be found at* wendynikel.wordpress.com/short-stories.

The Piper

Brenda Kezar

The stranger followed the dirt road into the heart of the run-down little village and paused in the lengthening shadows of the buildings lining the street. Not a soul in sight. The village looked uninhabited, but he knew better. His gaze fell on the closest building: a pub.

"Good fate intervenes." He smiled and crossed to it.

Inside, the pub was gloomy and dusty and twice as shabby as the village outside. Hazy oil lamps lined the walls and offered little light. The air smelled of stale beer, sweat, and cheap tobacco, but the bottles lining the wall behind the counter looked well used, and the tables looked clean enough.

The barkeep, broom in hand, stepped through a door behind the counter. His eyes fell on the stranger and he frowned. "We were just closing."

"We?" Every table sat empty, and there was no sign of any other staff but the barkeep. The stranger sighed and pulled out a chair. "Look. I've had a long journey. I'd like—*I need*—a glass of ale to wash the road dust from my mouth. I won't keep you long."

The barkeep scowled and leaned his broom against the wall. "Fine. One. But it better be quick. What'll ya have?"

"A tall glass of house ale, if you please." The stranger smiled and sat.

The barkeep set a glass in front of him and poured it half full. He set the bottle on the next table, just out of the stranger's reach, and trudged to the window. He looked out at the street, shook his head, and pulled the shutters tightly closed.

"You'll be needing a room," he said, matter-of-factly.

The stranger nodded. "If you could direct me to the nearest inn—."

"It's too late, the sun has set. But lucky for you, I've got a room upstairs." He dropped a heavy beam across the door. "Else you'd be sleeping on a table."

"Lucky me." The stranger drained his glass and eyed the bottle. "Since we're stuck for the night anyway, how about another?"

The barkeep weighed the idea. "Might as well. A shilling is a shilling." He refilled the stranger's glass — full, this time.

"Your little village doesn't offer much in the way of nightlife, does it?" The stranger sat back in his chair and basked in the warmth the ale brought to his road-weary muscles.

"We roll up the streets at sunset *because* of the nightlife. Ghastly things lurk in the dark." He lit the candle on the stranger's table and then circled the room, snuffing the lamps, until the single candle remained the only light. "The light draws them."

The stranger cleared his throat. "That's actually why I'm here. I believe I might be of service."

The barkeep goggled at him for a heartbeat, then brayed with laughter. "Think you can, do you? I'd wager you can't. No one can. We've tried them all, and all have failed." His face went serious. "We are damned."

The stranger sipped his drink. "How did it happen?"

"It was the mayor's doing. Him and the damn council." He spat into the litter of tobacco, dirt, and nutshells scattered on the floor. "The plague came. Bodies filled the streets. You couldn't open your shutters for the reek of the dead. Our own gravedigger, exhausted and overworked, caught it and died. The gravedigger from the next town — a Romany, if you can believe it — offered to take on the task. Did a damn fine job, too, but the village council still refused to pay. The Romany cursed our village: forever more, our dead will not *need* a gravedigger. Our dead will rise and walk, and they will prey upon the living."

The stranger frowned. "When they saw his curse had come true, why didn't they pay him?"

"It was too late. He'd caught the plague himself and died with the curse still in place." He cocked his head and listened, his eyes wide. "They come," he whispered.

Outside, there was a slow scraping sound, like someone dragging one weak leg behind them. A low moaning accompanied the scraping, like wind groaning in the trees. Something growled, and the shuffling noise multiplied, as if a whole herd of leg-draggers filled the street. There was another growl and an answering snarl. The moaning grew louder. Whatever it was, it — or they — were coming toward the pub doors. The stranger and the barkeep watched the door and held their breath.

Something thumped against the door and they both jumped. The door banged again, hard enough to make the beam rattle. A shower of dust sifted down from the rafters on to the stranger's table. He and the barkeep looked at each other.

After a few heartbeats of silence, the moaning and shuffling noises resumed, moving away. The barkeep turned to the stranger, his eyes wide, his face gray. "I'd be finishing up that drink, if I were you," he whispered. He jerked his head toward the door he'd come through earlier. "Your room is through that door, up the stairs." He turned and slunk toward the door himself.

The next morning, the stranger met with the mayor and the village council in the Great Hall. The Great Hall looked as if it had once been a great church but had fallen on hard times: most of the pews were missing, the stained glass gone, and the windows covered with dirty, rotting boards. Mortar dust and chunks of disintegrated brick scrunched beneath his feet. The whole thing looked as if it might collapse at any moment.

Where the altar should have been, a long, ornate oak table sat. The mayor sat in the middle chair, and the four council members flanked him. The stranger stood before them like a penitent seeking judgment.

"Don't be ridiculous." The mayor rolled his eyes. "We've tried everything. No one can rid us of the undead."

Councilman Breman studied the stranger. "How do you propose to rid us of the problem?"

"You can't seriously think —," the mayor interrupted. A sharp look from Breman silenced him.

The piper smiled. He pulled a flute from the pack at his hip and held it up. "With this."

The councilmen looked at each other and burst out laughing.

"You mean to beat them over the head with it, or stab it into their unbeating hearts?" The mayor laughed.

The stranger waited patiently for the laughter to die. "Neither. I propose to play a magical tune and lead them away from your good village forever, never to return."

Councilman Breman shook his head. "That's ridiculous."

"I *can* do it," the stranger said. "And to prove it, no payment will be required until I have accomplished the feat."

The mayor shook his head and waved the stranger away. "Enough. I've no time for —."

"Quiet," Breman snapped. He stroked his chin. "And just what payment would you require for this service, should it actually work?"

"My weight in gold."

One of the councilmen whistled. "A steep price," Breman said.

"Yes," the stranger said, "but isn't it worth it to be rid of the undead plague?"

"I object!" The mayor leapt to his feet, his cheeks flushed. "This is preposterous. Why —."

"Sit down!" Breman roared. The mayor's mouth snapped shut and he sank back into his seat. "Why not?" Breman continued, more gently. "What can it hurt to try? If he fails, we owe him nothing. Correct?"

"Absolutely correct." The stranger nodded and bowed.

"Fine, Mister . . ." Breman paused, searching for a name the stranger hadn't given.

The stranger smiled. "You may call me Piper."

"Fine, Mr. Piper," Breman said. "Work your magic. And if you rid the village of the undead, you will receive your weight in gold."

"Thank you. I promise you won't be disappointed." He bowed and turned to leave, but paused. "One more thing. I want to warn you, I am not someone you want to cheat."

The mayor leapt to his feet and slammed his fist against the desk. "What are you accusing us of?"

The Piper held up his hand. "Not an accusation, a warning. Do not cheat me, good sirs. If you cheat me, I will make your current undead plague seem like a blessing. You have been warned."

He strode out the door and left the council staring after him.

The Piper stood in the center of the road, flute in hand, and watched the sun sink behind the buildings. In the houses that lined the street, villagers with anxious faces stood in windows and doorways. As the sun sank lower, more and more villagers gave up the watch. The street echoed with the banging of shutters, the slamming of doors, and the thudding of beams being dropped into place. As the shadows of the buildings lengthened, touched, then faded away, he found himself alone.

In the dusky gloom they came. One appeared in the distance, shuffling and jerking along the road toward him. Another appeared behind it, and then several more. Their shuffling, jerking feet raised puffs of dust as they came to him, the only living thing left on the streets. The lead undead spotted him and let out a slow, sad moan that made the hair on his arms stand up, and it shuffled faster toward him. By the time it was close enough to make out the features of its face—dark hair, gray-green skin, tattered black trousers—a herd of one hundred undead shuffled and moaned behind it.

The Piper drew in a deep breath and raised his flute. He began to play a slow, sad melody. The undead herd stopped and cocked their heads. He picked up the tempo and broke into a happy, jaunty tune, and the closest undead began to bob its head in time. He smiled and fumbled a note but quickly recovered. The undead herd bobbed their heads in unison, keeping perfect time.

The Piper turned and walked away, still playing the jaunty tune. The undead followed him, shuffling slowly, heads bobbing, a happy parade of rotting corpses.

He looked over his shoulder and smiled, and this time he didn't miss a note. He led them down the road and out of the village, toward the blue and white mountains in the distance.

Two days later, The Piper returned to the Great Hall. He stepped up to the table and bowed. "Gentleman, I believe you will find my services have been satisfactory. I weigh twelve stone, but I will not be offended if you wish to make measure of my weight yourself."

"Don't be ridiculous," the mayor waved his hand. "We don't have that much gold."

The Piper looked from the mayor to the council. "I beg your pardon? I named my price and you agreed. I kept my end of the bargain. I expect you to keep yours."

"And just what have you done that we should pay you?" The mayor asked.

"Have you all gone mad?" The Piper narrowed his eyes. "You know what I've done. I've rid your village of the undead plague."

The mayor laughed and laid his finger to his cheek coyly. "Undead plague? Impossible! There's no such thing."

The Piper's eyes met Breman's. "Do you not remember the lesson of the undertaker?"

The Mayor scowled and shook his head. "We have no idea what you're talking about." The councilmen fidgeted under the Piper's glare and wouldn't meet his eyes.

Councilman Breman cleared his throat. "John, perhaps there is some way —."

The Mayor held up his hand. "Quiet. I will not entertain the ravings of a con man. He is obviously insane." He leaned over the table and glowered at the Piper. "Undead plague, indeed. What nonsense! Leave immediately, or I will have you put in the stocks."

The Piper put his hands on his hips and stood tall. "Then you will not be paying me?"

"Of course not." The mayor crossed his arms and leaned back in his chair.

"Then I guess I shall take my payment some other way." The Piper spun and stormed toward the door. As his hand touched the door handle, he looked over his shoulder, a half-smile playing on his lips. "You can't say you weren't warned."

⚜

Two days later, the mayor woke to shouting in the streets. His first thought was the undead were back, but the early morning sunlight streaming through the window set his mind at ease: the undead never came in daylight.

He jumped out of bed and threw open the window. Below, a crowd had gathered. "What's going on?" he asked.

"The children. They are missing!" Mr. Goodwell's face was pinched and worried. Beside him, his wife sobbed into her hands.

"Ours, too," Mr. Flannery added. His wife sat in the dust, her face buried in her hands. Others in the crowd murmured in agreement. All the children of the village were missing.

The mayor sent a messenger to gather the council for a special meeting at the Great Hall. When he arrived, the council members were already waiting outside the heavy doors, silently fidgeting, their faces ashen. Many of them had missing children themselves, but that was not the reason for their worried expressions: a knife held a note to the heavy wooden doors.

The note read: *Our debt is settled. Signed, The Piper.*

The councilmen and the mayor exchanged worried glances.

"Why would he steal our children?" one wailed.

"What does he intend to do with them?" another whispered, his eyes wide.

"I knew we should have rendered payment!" Breman snapped. "John, this is all your fault."

"Everyone, settle down," the mayor said. "He can't have gone far, not with a mass of captives. We will send out search parties. Rest assured, we will have our children back by nightfall."

But by the third day, no one could find the Piper or the children. No one could even find so much as a footprint in the mud to show which direction the Piper had gone.

In desperation, messengers were sent to hang notices in the surrounding villages: "Beware the Piper" the notices said, and, "Reward for the Capture of the Piper."

Two weeks after the children disappeared, the townspeople milled in the road at dusk, commiserating their sorrow as they had every night since the children disappeared. They gathered in small knots, talking in low, sad voices, dabbing at their eyes with handkerchiefs.

Mr. Goodman crossed the street, meaning to give his condolences again to Mr. Pokerwoski, when something caught his eye. In the distance, at the farthest edge of the village, a small silhouette walked the road toward them. Another small figure appeared behind it. It was too dark to make out who they were, but Mr. Goodman knew in his heart.

"Praise God!" Mr. Goodman shouted and pointed. "The children are back."

Everyone rushed to the center of the street, their eyes wide in disbelief, their faces filled with hope.

The two children came closer. More children fell in behind them.

The townspeople clapped with delight. Men slapped each other on the backs, women hugged and danced in circles. "They're back! The Piper has returned our babes!"

They crowded together and rushed to meet the children. Too late, they realized the moaning and shuffling noises were back.

Brenda Kezar *is a horror and fantasy writer from North Dakota. Her short stories have appeared in Silverthought, Bonded by Blood V, Penumbra eMag, A High Shrill Thump, Inclinations, Down in the Cellar, Thema, Emerald Tales, Loving the Undead, and Zombidays: Festivities of the Flesheaters. You can find her on the web at:* www.BrendaKezar.com.

www.ingramcontent.com/pod-product-compliance
Lightning Source LLC
Chambersburg PA
CBHW051257170626
46809CB00004B/1687